PART-TIME POSER

Royally Wed Romantic Comedy: Book 3

PAMELA DUMOND

Pamela DuMond Media

Part-time Poser

(Royally Wed Romantic Comedy, #3)

ISBN: 978-1-941731-08-6

Published by Pamela DuMond Media

ALSO BY PAMELA DUMOND

'HOT' ROMANCE

21st CENTURY COURTESAN series

TYCOON: A 21st Century Courtesan Prologue
PLAYER #1
MOVIE STAR #2
BELOVED #3 - Coming soon
HUSBAND #4 - Coming soon

THE CROWN AFFAIR series

His Sexy Cinderella - A Crown Affair Prologue
The Prince's Playbook #1
His Majesty's Measure #2
The American Princess #3
The Duchess's Decision #4

❧

PLAYING DIRTY ROM-COM Stand Alones

The Client
The Matchmaker

❧

'SWEETER' ROMANCE

ROYALLY WED ROM-COM series

Part-time Princess #1 —Licensed as a CHAPTERS Interactive
Stories Game.
Royally Wed #2
Part-time Poser #3
Royally Knocked Up #4

❧

PLAYING SWEETER ROM-COM Stand Alones

Ms. Match Meets a Millionaire
The Story of You and Me

❧

MORTAL BELOVED TIME TRAVEL series

The Messenger #1
The Assassin #2
The Seeker #3
The Believer #4: Jack & Clara — *STAND ALONE*

COZY MYSTERIES

ANNIE GRACELAND COZY MYSTERIES

Cupcakes, Lies, and Dead Guys #1
Cupcakes, Sales, and Cocktails
Cupcakes, Pies, and Hot Guys
Cupcakes, Paws, and Bad Santa Claus
Cupcakes, Diaries, and Rotten Inquiries
Cupcakes, Bats, and Scaredy Cats
Cupcakes, Bars, and Rock Stars
Cupcakes, Spies, and Despicable Guys - Also available to play
as a **Chapters Interactive Stories Game .**
Cupcakes, Screams, and Drama Queens - Coming soon

NON-FICTION

Staying Young: Simple Techniques to Look and Feel Young

For

Caitlyn O'Leary

Your big, kind heart.
Your hilarious sense of humor.

Keywords.

ABOUT THIS BOOK

PRAISE for Royally Wed Romantic Comedy

Five Stars **"Why can't I be a Part-Time Princess?!**
Amazing, I loved this book!!"** ~ London Dreaming

Five Stars "Absolutely **Freaking Hi - lar - ri - ous!!!**" ~ Avid
Reader923

Four Stars "This is a **flirty fun read."** ~ Karen's Book Haven

Five Stars "AHHHHH **I LOVELOVELOVE** this Book!" ~
Maryam Dinzly

Five Stars **"Pamela's books are like potato chips,** you
cannot read just one..." Jenny James

DESCRIPTION

I used to be a cocktail waitress but then I married Prince

Nicholas of Fredonia -- he of the abs so ripped I mend them with my tongue every night.

Now my life's practically a party filled with hot romance, glitter and glam, and, *and...*

What do you mean Nick and I aren't legally wed?

The Archbishop claims our wedding was performed by a charlatan, a poser priest. If the paparazzi gets ahold of this they'll rip the royal family's reputation to shreds.

Nick's got obligatory guard duty so I'm traveling to Venice, Italy with Prince Cristoph and my party-hard Ladies-in-Waiting to track down the poser and shut this problem down now.

What could possibly go wrong?

CHAPTER 1

"I don't understand," I said, pacing back and forth across the living room of the spectacularly appointed red brick townhouse in the capital city of Sauerhausen, Fredonia. Our gorgeous new home was a pricey piece of property situated next door to Crown Prince Cristoph's posh pad. I looked out the two-story floor to ceiling windows straight into picturesque Centralaski Park, night lights beaming low in the fogged air above the running path that circled the pond in the near distance. "It's like being a little bit pregnant. You're knocked up or you're not. We're married or we're not."

"Hell yes, we're married, Lucy," Prince Nicholas said. "Stop worrying! The nightmare, otherwise known as *getting* married, is in the rearview. Everything is in order. Everything is in place."

"Says the man who had three couches delivered to the new home but can't make up his mind which one he wants."

The enormous sofas: one a rich chocolate brown tufted leather, another a crimson velvet pudding couch, and the third a sturdy, sensible tapestry, rested uncomfortably next to each other in the cavernous living room. They resembled in-laws from opposite sides of the family that didn't like each other all that much, who had been corralled together for a family holiday.

If I had to vote for a favorite sofa right now, it would be the one on which Prince Nicholas Frederick Timmel of Fredonia was currently sprawled. He wore jeans and a long-sleeved T-shirt that clung to his well-toned chest and back, highlighting his buff, built arms. A two-day shadow bristled on his face, and his thick black hair bordered on the longish side. One muscular hand absent-mindedly scratched our dog Tulip's head. The yellow Labrador retriever gazed off into the distance as if the prince had hypnotized her, or perhaps fed her too many liver treats. Prince Nicholas of Fredonia was sexy as sin, and—in my humble opinion—good with tricks as well as treats.

"Minor details." He smiled at me and beckoned with his index finger. "At the end of the day this confusion will most likely be revealed as a clerical mistake. Let's attend to the important matter. Which sofa do we pick for our new living room? I'm kind of leaning toward this one right now." He patted the leather seat cushion next to him, as Tulip hopped off, stretched in down dog, and lumbered toward the kitchen. "Come over here, let's get naked, give it a go, and see what it's really made of. We can't pick a wuss of a couch for, god's sakes. What kind of standards would we set for our children?"

"You mean our dog?" I watched Tulip disappear around the corner into the kitchen, her tail wagging from her hairy behind like a metronome.

"Today it's the dog. Tomorrow it's children," Nick said. "Strong moral convictions, Lucy, start with the parents. I say we start here and now. You and me. Raising the bar. Setting standards." He patted the leather again, and then gave it a suggestive slap. "While we do the naked horizontal happy dance."

"I can't have sex on a leather sofa right now. I'm a practical girl and I need to make sense of this kerfuffle."

I ignored his beckoning finger and stomped back and forth across the rich, honey-toned natural woods lining the floors. Nick had purchased the new townhouse two weeks ago, before I marched down the aisle at the St. Francis of Assisi chapel. Before we were royally wed. Before some smartass, know-it-all fancy-robed guy wearing a bejeweled pointy hat, stamped "Null and Void" all over my marriage certificate and should have just stamped it all over my heart.

The Archbishop Causesdesperdues left me not knowing for sure if I was married or not married to the handsomest man in the world, the Prince of Fredonia, the sexy, adorable smartass who had captured my heart and put a ring on my significant finger.

"Aha. I knew it," Nick said. "You're too soft-hearted to go for the leather. I saw you bonding with the cows when we visited the Grand Duke's estate in Edelweiss." He stood up and walked over to the pudding sofa. He plopped down on it and put his feet up on the only coffee table in the room. "You stroked Flopsie's head and said, 'Don't let them tell you this is only women's work. Get the rest of the girls together, form a union, and then you'll be a force to be reckoned with.'" He ran his hand back and forth over the red velvet. "You're simply too in touch with the animals. Perhaps you'd prefer this one? I suspect it's a cotton blend. It's soft, sensuous to the touch, and yet firm—just like you."

"Well, those girls *should* band together," I said. "Women are always working their asses off and still getting eighty cents on every dollar made by a man. For god's sake, we live in modern times, and the gender gap is ridiculously medieval." I peeked out the windows at the snow-capped French Alps in the distance and could almost make out the town of Friedricksburgh high in the foothills above the city. The postcard-perfect small town that was the site of my last two wedding attempts.

My first walk down the aisle was here in Sauerhausen at the Royal Cathedral in an attempt to marry the wrong guy, Nick's brother, Prince Cristoph. To my credit, at the last minute I copped to being a princess impersonator and said, "I don't" instead of "I do." To my chagrin, I made it all the way down the aisle before I decided to blow my own cover, and out myself as a phony, a fraud, a charlatan. That I was not Lady Elizabeth Billingsley, to the manner born, but instead Lucy Trabbicio, former cocktail waitress from the Southside of Chicago.

"In the name of détente, I request that you bring that hot ass of yours over here, Lucy," Nick said. He picked up the remote and aimed it at the flatscreen mounted high on the wall as he bounced up and down a few times on the cushions. "This piece seems well constructed. One can sit back and comfortably watch TV. But will it rock the Casbah factor?"

"How can I worry about the Casbah factor when I don't know if we're married? We still haven't gotten word from either the Archbishop Causesdesperdues or the state. I feel like I was hit by a cement truck, and dragged a hundred feet by that cold-hearted man and his stupid cape."

"I will not allow men in capes to take you away from me." Nick sprang to his feet and walked a few steps toward me. He captured my hand and pulled me flush against him. "Step aside Superman. Move over Dracula. Be gone Archbishop Causesdesperdues. You, Lucy, are mine." He tugged the clip from my messy bun, tossing it, and weaving his fingers through my long hair. He leaned in and kissed me on the lips. Hot. Long. Wet. Delicious.

Good God, the man could sell ice to Eskimos.

I reluctantly ripped myself from his smoldering lips and glanced up at him. "A guy who sends you a telegram while you're on your honeymoon to inform you that you're not married is not 'Superman,' I air quoted. "I prefer to call him 'Bully Man,' or 'Rain on Your Parade' man. Besides, I dare anyone to try and take *you* away from *me*.

I journeyed down the wedding aisle the *second* time at the Royal Chapel in Friedricksburgh on my way to marry the *right* prince—his royal gorgeousness, Nicholas. But I was ditched, a bride left standing alone in front of the altar without a groom, holding a kiss-off note in one bejeweled hand. "What kind of mean people kidnap a man on his wedding day? Thank God, my Ladies-in-Waiting and I were able to track you down and rescue you."

"Color me eternally grateful, Lucy. How embarrassing that the kidnappers stuffed me blindfolded and zip-tied in the basement of some pretty-in-pink wedding planning joint. I thank my lucky stars every day that the paparazzi didn't snap photos and plaster them everywhere. That reminds me: I've been meaning to talk with you about the blindfolded thing. I recently saw a documentary on cable about..."

"Not now, Nick." I gazed into his crystal blue eyes and smoothed a lock of black hair off his forehead. "I didn't think I'd ever say this to you, but your cheekbones are looking a bit sharper these days. Did those horrible Weddings R Us people at least give you water and feed you?"

"Briny water and stale bread for three solid days, Lucy. It's a wonder I survived. I'm still traumatized wife, and I need soothing. Take off your clothes and have your wicked ways with me. Fuck me silly, Lucy, before it's too late, and all hope is lost."

"Fine," I sighed, kicking off my Uggs. "But only because I hate bullies. I'll put up with a random asshole, flip the bird at an obnoxious driver, but bullies push me over the edge. Speaking of, I'm going to track down that nasty, petty arch-bishop, and stamp 'null and void' all over his head until he issues us a new marriage certificate. That's the only way I know this thing will get resolved. If you want something done right, you do it yourself." I yanked off my socks and pitched those on the floor as well.

"I have a better way for you to blow off steam, my love." Nick slipped his hand under my blouse, his fingers sliding up my stomach invoking tingling sensations that zipped down and performed cartwheels over my private girlie parts.

"We can't have sex on the leather couch," I said. "I don't think we can return it if we have sex on it."

"I know, darling. We're having sex on the velvet one. I'm doing this for your own good, my love. I'm on a mission." Nicholas dropped to his knees, pressing his lips against my stomach and nibbled my skin. The scruff of his black shadow was both rough and ticklish as he pushed my shirt up higher. His fingers grazed the hand-spun black lace of my bra, curving over the swell of my breast.

My breath hitched as his muscular hands dropped to either side of my waist, grasped the top of my pelvic bones and abruptly swiveled my hips to face him. "Whoa! Slow up Ranger Danger!" I said, staring down at him. "Whiplash!"

"That's Captain Danger to you. Besides, it's whiplash you'll write home about," he said, lightly slapping me on my ass, pulling me to him and sinking his lips onto my stomach. His breath was warm and moist against my bare skin as he trailed kissed down my abdomen.

Heat flushed through my body like I'd walked into the steam room at the local YMCA and I had a pretty good idea where his mouth was headed. "What does this mission entail?

"Search and Rescue. I'm still on the search part." He tickled me, and I burst out laughing.

No matter how stressed out I was, Nicholas always found a way to make me smile. This is why we worked. This is why I fell in love with him. This is why I was willing to fight for him. I smiled. "You missed a spot." I pointed to the top button on my jeans.

"I'm sorry, spot," he said, unbuttoning them with patient fingers one by one, lingering between buttons to work his tongue lower. "Please don't hold it against me." He stopped, and tugged my jeans down over my hips, wriggling them down my legs.

"Spot forgives you," I said, kicking them off.

"I love you, Lucy." His teeth snagged the top edge of the lace of my bikini bottoms and he dragged them down over the tops of my thighs.

"How did I score such a hot guy?"

Tulip barked in the kitchen.

"I haven't scored yet, Lucy. But it's bottom of the ninth, I'm rounding the bases, and heading toward home. I swear I can hear the crowds chanting my name."

"That's Tulip. I think she has to make a potty. I *know* Mother's precious, yum-yum dog!" I hollered. "Dinner time soon, I promise." But she barked and whined again, her claws scraping against our front door. "She's hungry. Maybe we should—"

"I just fed her half a package of liver treats. Besides, I'm hungry too. We should do exactly what we're doing." Nick's lips headed further south, prompting me to change my mind and wholeheartedly agree with him.

"Holy crap you're good at that." My head was spinning and I tried to remember how to breathe.

"I know." He came up for air and glanced up at me, a sexy smile on his face. "I trained in high school you know."

"You did not. Stop exaggerating and get back to business."

"I did. I was certified in Scuba in the deep end of the pool. That does wonders for a man's breathing abilities," he said and then, luckily for me, got back to business.

As much as I hated the beauty makeover I'd endured after

I accepted my new part-time job working impersonating a royal lady—color me grateful for the whole waxing ordeal. Eighteen months ago I was an impoverished cocktail waitress, fired from my job at MadDog Biker Bar, desperate to keep my Uncle John at his pricy Vail Assisted Living Care Facility on Chicago's Southside. I answered an Internet work for hire listing on Daveslist and accepted a part-time job impersonating Lady Elizabeth Billingsley.

"Lizzie" had hired me to 'babysit' Crown Prince Cristoph Timmel, fly to Fredonia, and keep him on the straight and narrow in the small jewel of a country tucked next to Monaco and France in the French Alps. She had planned on returning to Fredonia, and to Cristoph's side in five days tops to accept his marriage proposal.

I quickly discovered this job paid extremely well, but it wasn't the easiest work in the world. I was subjected to a terrifying makeover in which I was aggressively groomed, forced to shop at high end department stores and boutiques, schooled to walk in high heels, and tutored on how to homogenize my vowels in order to refine my Chicago accent. I earned every pound and pence these tight-assed Fredonia royals paid me.

I sailed through my makeover with flying colors. Okay—except for the body-waxing thing—which to this day terrifies me. I practiced *not* looking for red clearance sales tags, studied up on spoon placement, and memorized the names and relationships of all the important players in Elizabeth's life, including the Royal Fredonia family.

I had it all going on. I was boss. I was "such a nasty woman" even a bombastic politician would have called me out. But then the whole plan was blown sky high like vaped medicinal marijuana mist. It happened a few minutes after I boarded the flight bound from Chicago to London Heathrow, my first official step on the physical journey to Fredonia as Lady Elizabeth Billingsley's imposter.

My hair was coiffed, my makeup perfect, and I wore my new Chanel suit and carried my matching bag as I claimed my seat in first class cabin on British Air, seat 4B. I might have looked cool but I was totally sweating whether I'd be able to successfully pull off my Elizabeth impersonation. I hadn't planned on Prince Nicholas Frederick Timmel of Fredonia who sat down in the seat next to me.

No one warned me that Nick and Elizabeth had a sexual history. If we really wanted to get honest, no one even warned me that Nick was Crown Prince Cristoph's younger brother by 10 months. Both men were devastatingly handsome, womanizers, and forces to be reckoned with. So it wasn't really my fault that my eyes were diverted from the prize, Prince Cristoph, and landed squarely on his younger brother, Nicholas, he of the sharp cheekbones, dark hair, blue eyes and nickel sized cleft in his chin.

I tried to resist, really I did, but I fell hard for the irresistible bad boy, the incorrigible flirt. Shortly after I bolted from The Royal Fredonia Cathedral in Sauerhausen after I said "I don't" instead of "I do" during my marriage attempt to Prince Cristoph, Nick tracked me down to Chicago and proposed to the real me, Lucy Trabbicio. Because wonder of wonders he'd fallen in love—*hard*— with the real me as well.

Tulip barked again. I heard a strange scraping, sound and a gust of chilly wind blew into our place and extinguished the candles next to the fireplace. "Yes, Tulip. Give your dog mother a few more precious mommy minutes. I'll be there soon. Then it will be all the organic venison kibble you want."

But she barked again, high and sharp, anxious and demanding.

"Yes, Tulip. Soon!" I exclaimed, one of my legs splayed across the top of the red velvet sofa, the heel on my other foot dug into the couch's extra wide and comfortable cushion. I noticed my toenails painted in purple, gold, and white— Fredonia's royal accent colors— as my toes curled with Nick's every thrust, and every well positioned move. I couldn't help but think this might indeed be the couch for us.

"Yes, yes, Lucy!" Nick cried out.

"Oh, holy, crap!" I exclaimed, and dug my fingernails into the rich red velvet cotton blend.

"Oh, holy, crap!" A female voice said from the inside of our apartment. "This place is spectacular!"

Nick's eyes popped open directly over my face. "Did you invite your ladies over?"

"No! I don't consider this a spectator sport—yet."

"Nicholas. You're bouncing up and down on that couch just like you used to do on the spare bed in the guest quarters at the royal palace. Why aren't you wearing any underwear, my adorable grandson? I guess I know what I'm getting you for Christmas. Smile for the camera!"

"My grandmother!" Nick boomeranged off me like he'd been hit in the eye with a flying tennis ball. "My grandmother is taking pictures of us shagging!"

CHAPTER 2

Her Royal Highness was eighty-six-years-old, and looked every second of it as she squinted at me from across our flat. She was bent over her walker, one hand petting Tulip, the other holding her smart phone high in the air clicking pictures of our new townhouse.

"Hello, Royal Nana," I said, and sunk, panicked, back into the deepest recesses of the pudding couch. "Lovely to see you. No pictures please. Were we expecting you?" I glanced around and spotted my jeans and long-sleeved light pink fleece shirt tossed onto the floor, not remotely within reaching distance.

Nick crawled away, grabbed his pants, crouched behind the wing of the sofa, and wriggled them on.

"Wuss!" I mouthed, glaring at him.

"It should be perfectly obvious I've come for a pint of lager, my darling new grand-daughter-in law or whatever you are. And to snap a few photos of your new abode to share on my official Facebook page."

"We're not ready to share pictures of our new flat on social media yet," I said, glaring at Nick as he hurriedly pulled on his shirt and buttoned it up. I pointed one judgmental finger at my clothes lying in a heap on the ground that were too far for me to reach, but were well within his grasp. "Toss them to me," I whispered, extending my hand. "Now!"

"That's too bad," Royal Nana said, still holding her phone in the air as she rolled forward with her walker, a crocheted purple, gold, and white afghan draped over the front bar. "Spacious interiors. Lovely. Please don't clutter them up right away." *Click.* "Cottage Stone fireplace. Nice touch. Don't forget to wipe down the grout every now and again." *Click.* "Fantastic view of Centralaski Park." *Click. Click. Click.* "It looks practically identical to Cristoph's place. You could have just moved in with him."

"Same architect, I believe," Nick said.

"Cristoph is still a bachelor, Nana," I said. "We're a married couple, need our own space, and will be decorating accordingly. Why don't you wait until we've completely unpacked before you take pictures? In fact, I think you should come back next week when our flat is more put together, and take as many photos as you like." I snapped my fingers at Nick and pointed again to my clothes.

"The tabloids, can't seem to decide your marital status, and you know me, I hate all that gossipy crap, and was hoping to allay their suspicions. Lucy, I can't get a good picture of you down there. Poke your head up from that couch so I can snap a decent photo."

"I'd love to, Nana, but I'm makeup free today. Airing out the skin." More like airing out *all the skin.* "No pictures for me."

"Later then," she said, rolling toward me like the Russians advancing on Berlin at the end of World War II. "Christmas season will soon be upon us. Plenty of time for holiday cheer as well as photo ops. I've brought a house-warming present for you, and now that I've sized the place up, I think it will fit perfectly on the accent wall next to the fireplace." She stopped and furrowed her brows. "Why do you have so many couches?"

"We're trying them on for size, Nana," Nick said, snagging my jeans, and lobbing them in my direction. They flew high through the air and sailed over the couch, landing on the pedestal claw foot of the large rectangular wooden dining table. "Sorry," he mouthed, shrugging his shoulders.

"Sorry doesn't cut it," I whispered, slapping a hand on my forehead. But my boobs bounced freely, and I realized that they, as well as the rest of my pink parts, would momentarily be in Nana's camera range.

"You're a sensible young man, Nicholas. You get that from my side of the family. Not that airhead American actress mother of yours. The royal gossips whisper sweet nothings in my ears trying their best to suck up to me so I'll support their cause du jour," Royal Nana said. "I told them all to sod off whenever they ask me how I feel that you and Lucy might not be married. About the sordid dilemma that the two of you are possibly living in sin."

"We're married," Nick said. "End of story."

"I'm sorry that they are hounding you," I said. "Just tell them this isn't the 1950s and living together is normal, not sordid. Perhaps this isn't the best time to visit? In fact, let's set up a date next week after we decide on a couch. I'll make real eggnog. Nick, escort your grandmother to her vehicle, please."

"Come on, Nana. I'll make sure you are safely tucked back into your town car," Nick said, lifting my lace undies and pitching them in my direction.

I shot my hand up like a ball player. But once again, he'd overthrown and they flew inches above my fingers. "No!"

"No what?" Nana asked.

Tulip barked, crouched, and leaped into the air. She

caught my thong in her teeth, shook it violently, and dropped it in front of the walker. She collapsed onto her stomach on the hardwoods, and wagged her tail in anticipation that Nana would pick it up and throw it for her again.

"No... we wouldn't want you to trip over something a thoughtless carpenter left behind," I said.

"You have an interesting carpenter," Royal Nana said, staring down at my undies. "Posh, it's a perfect time to visit. Besides, Nicholas popped over to my chateau on Friday, vacuumed, took out the trash, and rubbed my shoulders. I asked him when I could see the new fancy-pants townhouse. He said, 'Drop by any time this weekend. We have no commitments or solid plans.' Right, my favorite grandson?"

"Um... I was thinking you'd call first," Nick said.

An ancient man trod into the flat carrying a thin six foot by four foot cardboard container.

"Herr Fingerlachen!" Nana thrust her arthritic hand in the air in his direction, "Did you not hear Nicholas say we could stop by *anytime* this weekend in the afternoon?"

"Yes, Your Royal Highness." He deposited it on the floor, took a moment to catch his breath, and rubbed his hands together. "A bit of a nip in the air tonight. Splendid place you have here. The fireplace is roaring. Are those chestnuts roasting? I do love a toasty fire on a chilly night. Can I safely leave Her Royal Highness's house-warming gift on this wall, or will it damage the paint?"

"Lean away," Nick said.

"No," I said. "He needs to lean away on a different day."

"Yes, Lucille," Fingerlachen said. "It is a splendid day." He rested the package against the wall and stiffly shrugged off his overcoat.

I shot dagger eyes at Nick. "Get rid of them," I whispered, suddenly realizing that the thought of my clothes magically flying through the air, landing on top of me, and covering my nakedness was tragically, only a fantasy. I glanced around looking for coverage of sorts, but only a bag of chips and the TV remote were within reach. I grabbed the bag of spicy BBQ Ridge-cut kettle chips, slapped them on top of my lower girlie parts, and the remote over my boobs but it only semi-covered the left one.

"Allow me to help you, Herr Fingerlachen," Nick said, hustling over to the man and hanging his coat on the reclaimed barn door peg rack protruding from the foyer wall.

"So glad you can help *him*," I said, squeezing my tatas together between my arms hoping the remote would cover both. But I only resembled a pin-up girl perfect inspiration for a horny, desperate, gadget-geek pervert.

"Don't get up for me, Lucy," Nana said, rolling forward on her march toward world domination and townhouse conquering. "Although I'm sure you're on pins and needles wondering what your house warming gift is."

"That I am." Perhaps her eyesight was shot and she hadn't yet seen that I was naked. I placed my other hand casually over my other breast, contemplating if I should drop my foot that still rested on top of the sofa's back but feared I might upset the strategic chip bag placement. Instead, I concentrated on looking nonchalant; and I have no idea how—managed to hit a button on the remote, changing the TV channel on the flatscreen that hung over the fireplace.

"Except for the three couches your place is even better than I imagined. Why are you naked on the red velvet pudding sofa?" Royal Nana asked. "Never mind. I see you're watching porn."

Dramatic moans and groans emanated from the flatscreen TV. I glanced up and realized, that I'd hit a Triple X channel. I scrambled to punch a different button, but that involved angling the remote, and I didn't want to completely expose a boob. "Sorry! I *don't* make it a habit of watching porn in the early evening."

"Neither do I," she said, and plunked down on the leather couch perpendicular to the one I lay on. "I usually tune in around 10 pm. Have you seen that one show, *The Not So Young and the Feckless?* It's so realistic. Especially the nasty bits."

"No, I haven't seen that one." Nick's grandmother was here in our house, getting comfy on the sofa, settling in. Unless her Royal Highness died in the next few minutes, she was not going away any time soon. What could I do? "Nick can't wait to give you and Herr Fingerlachen the grand tour. Right, Nicholas?"

"Yes! Walk this way, Nana." Nick pointed to the tiny elevator next to the hall closet. "We can take the lift all the way to the rooftop garden. The city's Christmas lights are magical. The palace and the cathedral are completely lit up."

Royal Nana leaned back and stared at the screen. "That's not all that's lit up. I love this actor. Round firm buttocks. Chubby tallywacker. I'm tired. It wasn't easy driving here. Holiday traffic starts earlier every year you know. I'll take the tour another time. Herr Fingerlachen?"

"Yes, your Royal Highness."

"Come here and check out this couch. It's so sturdy." She patted the leather on the seat next to her and futzed with her walker, pulling the fuzzy afghan crocheted in the royal Fredonia colors onto her lap. "Nicholas, be a nice grandson, and bring us a few lagers and some snackies. Lucy appears a tad chilly." She tossed the afghan on top of me and winked.

"Yes, Nana," Nick said. He shot me a look, and shuddered.

"Greetings and salutations!" A female voice came from the doorway.

I shivered, pulling the small afghan on top of me.

"Google maps says I've arrived at my destination. Have I? Is this 11211 Centralaski Park West?"

"Duchess Edith of Friedricksburgh. Come on in you old bat." Royal Nana glanced back at the door as her frenemy entered our abode.

"Hello lovebirds!" Edith cooed. "Do you adore your new house-warming gift?"

"They haven't unwrapped it yet," Royal Nana said. "They've got plenty of couches for all of us, as well as chips and dip. We're watching porn. Like we always do at my place on Saturday nights."

"Splendid! You know how much I hate changing our routine."

My eyes met Nick's and I whispered, "Kill me now."

CHAPTER 3

Snowflakes wafted through the air, dusting our hair and warm winter coats on a Saturday afternoon as my ladies and I wandered Sauerhausen Old Town Farmer's Market. It was the second weekend in December and the Christmas/Hanukah holidays were already in full swing.

Twinkly holiday lights wrapped around trees and draped from the tops of gorgeous old buildings that resembled cake topper decorations in Sauerhausen, Fredonia's capital city. Holiday shoppers walked briskly through the urban streets as small bands consisting of three or four members played Christmas carols, and classic holiday standards like "White Christmas" and "Jingle Bells" outside shops as well as in bars and pubs. Despite the cornucopia of pressing world problems, there was still an undeniable holiday spirit in the air: hope, love, and longing for peace on Earth. Considering how cantankerous recent elections had been, I also suspected there was a desire for brandy-spiked eggnog, smooth single malt scotch, and schnapps with a kick of mint that simultaneously chilled one's throat and drowned one's sorrows.

We browsed the booths looking for presents, farm fresh groceries, and baked goods. Joan held a bar of homemade soap close to her nose and sniffed. "This has a hint of bacon. I might get distracted in the middle of showering and be tempted to eat it."

"As will your numerous shower mates," Esmeralda said.

"I'm not dating anyone," Joan replied. "I shower alone."

"Not for long," Esmeralda said. "Who doesn't love bacon?"

Joan waved a handful of Euros at the vendor. "I'll take five of these please."

"That booth on the far left is selling gingerbread crèches," Lady Cheryl Cavitt Carlson said, her hand flying to her heart. "The Wise Men's hats are covered in jewel-toned sugar icing. Watch my girls for a second, please? Must. Have!" She squeezed through the crowd toward the display.

Cheryl's youngest daughter, Violet, yawned. "I'm tired."

"You're always tired," Diana said.

Esmeralda rolled her eyes and pointed to a kiosk ten yards away. "Oh look, there's a booth with unicorn mugs and T-shirts."

"Yay!" Violet and Diana exclaimed and raced toward it.

"Be nice to the girls, Esmeralda," I said. "We were kids once."

"I'm plenty nice. I'm just tired of holiday shopping."

"Me too. Look at all these shoppers. Grabby. Pushy. Always wanting another deal. Oh look, there's the Friedricks-burgh Chocolate Chateaux booth. I need to snag one more thing."

Wedragged our purchases up the walkway toward my new townhouse. I stuck the key in the door and pushed it open. Tulip bounded down the steps into the front yard, greeting us with a few excited barks before disappearing to the far side of the yard to make a potty. Violet and Diana blasted past us like giggle monsters, and made their way into the house.

"I'm starving." Violet said.

"No more sugar," Cheryl said, looking harried as she trod after them, with Joan and Esmeralda on her heels. "I put turkey slices in the fridge."

The royal guard was slumped on a stool next to a tall hedge lining the front of our property. He was twenty-something, tall, and reed thin. He kept a low profile, wearing plain clothes, stationed on the border of our courtyard and Prince Cristoph's place, next door. It seemed like he was always on duty and I suspected he was ordered to keep an eye on us as well. I hoped they paid him a bit more for his extra work, but knowing government bureaucracy they probably nickel and dimed him to death.

I reached into my recyclable bag and dug around until I found the package of warm, fresh, chocolate chip cookies that I'd just nabbed at the market. "Excuse me, officer. I'm embarrassed to say that I don't know your name."

He looked up at me. "Private Parker."

"Thank you, Private Parker, for all your terrific work. I know this isn't the easiest job. It's boring and you can't tell your mates the details of your employment as you're bound by a privacy order if you're on royal watch." I passed him the warm bag, the scent of sugar and chocolate wafting through the air. "I used to cocktail waitress, so I know what tedious labor feels like. This isn't sufficient compensation for all you do. It's just a small 'gratitude' present."

"Thank you, Ms. Trabbicio. You didn't have to do that. Can I help you and the ladies with your purchases?" He grabbed a few of the heavy bags we'd deposited on the walkway.

"*Ms.* Trabbicio?" I asked, feeling my eye twitch as its matching brow slammed up toward my hairline of its own accord. "You *do* know that Prince Nicholas and I are married now, right? Technically that makes me a "Missus,' even though that sounds terribly retro and provincial."

"I heard news of that Ms.," he said, hauling my bags up the steps, and depositing them inside the front door. "Would you like me to carry these into the kitchen for you?"

"No, you've already been so helpful."

First rule of becoming a newly minted royal: if you come from humble roots, never forget them. The citizens of Fredonia had nicknamed me Almost Fake Fredonia Princess with a Heart, even giving me the hashtag "#AFFPHeart" almost two years ago, after I bolted from the cathedral in a mad dash to not marry the *wrong* prince. They'd even signed a petition to make me an official Fredonia citizen. Their outpouring of love and concern meant the world to me, but sadly, as was often the case with these online appeals, the automatic citizenship thing never happened.

"Private Parker," I said. "You look awfully familiar. Have we met before?"

"I don't know, Ms."

"You mean, 'I don't know, Missus.'"

"Yes, Ms. Whatever you say."

"Missus."

"Yes, Ms. Missus."

Perhaps he had waxy ear build up, was otherwise audibly impaired, or simply stone-cold tired from the monotonous hours of guard duty. "You don't need to rest on formalities, soldier," I said. "And whatever you do, please, don't call me

Duchess, even though I'll be granted the designation Duchess of Friedricksburgh. Those titles sound so stuffy. Let's cut through the formality. Just call me Lucy."

He pulled a thin, folded up newspaper from his coat pocket, glanced at it, and then at me. "Yes, Ms. Lucy."

But something didn't feel right and I was hit with the same kind of clingy, icky sensation that happened when I accidentally walked into a spider web. I pointed to his newspaper. "Can I see that?" He reluctantly handed it over. I shook it out, held it in front of me, and recoiled when I saw the picture of me on the front cover under the fold. I made an immediate note to buy thicker under eye concealer as I read the headline that blared:

"LUCY TRABBICIO: DUCHESS-NO-LONGER?"

It felt like a knife sliced into my heart. I inhaled sharply and hiccupped. "Do you mind if I keep this?" I asked, digging through my purse for spare change to reimburse him, my hand trembling. I couldn't locate any coins but I latched onto a crisp Euro from the sleeve of my wallet.

"That's fine, Ms.," he said. "You don't need to pay me. Just keep it."

"But, it's not fine." My hand shook as I passed him the bill and I hiccupped again. "Honestly—it's not fine at all."

CHAPTER 4

"I thought this whole nightmare was going to go away." I'd tossed the newspaper on the coffee table so hard the priceless, antique crystal Santa surrounded by reindeer centerpiece rattled. It spooked me for a second, and I couldn't help but wonder if it was an evil omen that Santa had decided he was throwing in the towel and *not* coming to town this year.

"Yeah, good luck with that one," Esmeralda said, leaning back on the red velvet pudding couch that we'd finally decided upon, and scrolled through the Internet on her cell phone.

"It's the beginning of December and the Christmas holidays are breathing down our necks," I said. "Don't these journalist vultures ever take a break?"

"I hear they're running low on turkeys this year," Cheryl said. "The vultures might be next in line. They're big birds, and with the proper mix of seasonings they can be quite tasty. I've been researching festive dinners in Crete. We're spending the holidays there this year."

"I'd stick with the lamb," Joan said. "Mediterranean

cultures have multitudes of super yummy lamb recipes. Google recipes for chops with mint leaves on top."

"Cook the journalist vultures," I said. "Turn the oven to 'Broil', and roast them. Hand me a fork and I'll pick the meat from their carcasses until nothing is left but their stringy tendons and parched bones."

"Well, technically, love, that would make you a vulture as well," Esmeralda said. "Albeit one that has access to an oven. Why don't we just wish them hell and damnation, sue the ones that get too far out of line, and use our hard-earned money to go shopping instead? I've got my eye on a bag by that hot, up and coming designer, Gareth Trent."

"Ooh, Gareth Trent!" Joan said, grabbing her phone, and tapping in a Google search. "His jeweled beige suede Hobo bag with the zipper and the fringe is to die for. I must admit I lust after that." She held her phone out in front of her. "Is this the one?"

Esmeralda leaned in and checked it out. "No. I need the black Moroccan leather tote, not the beige Hobo."

"Good luck," Joan said. "I heard there was a six month waiting list for that one."

"Not for me. I know people," Esmeralda said. "I *am* people. Besides, I'll visit Gareth, the sorry bastard, in Italy if I have to. From Sauerhausen, it's just a hop, skip, and a jump."

"Take me with you," Joan implored. "I love Italy, especially in December. Christmas holidays, pageants, parades, shopping. It's like main-lining sugar."

"That reminds me of the time I visited Sardinia for a quick weekend getaway, and discovered the resort where I snagged a reservation was hosting the Versace Underwear Model Competition," Esmeralda said.

"Do you have photos?" Joan asked.

She nodded. "And videos. Everyone signed off. Copyright cleared. It'll cost you."

"But—I'm your friend."

"Which is why I'll give you the Friends and Family discount," Esmeralda said, scrolling through her phone. She smiled when she found the file. "Allow me to tempt you with a small taste."

Joan leaned in again. "Holy moly. That's a Christmas stocking I'd like hanging in my flat."

"I too love the Christmas season." Cheryl pulled angel figurines out of her recyclable shopping bag. "Look at the handmade ornaments I scored. They're matchstick figurines adorned with yarn hair. So creative!"

"Super cute, Cheryl," I said.

"They're small enough I can pop them in my suitcase when I travel with my husband and kids on the holidays."

"You can place them under your tree in Crete," I said.

"Diana stole the remote. Not fair!" Violet yelled from the second floor. "I hate her, mother!"

"Be nice to each other for an hour, I beg you. Mommy needs girlfriend time." Cheryl frowned up at the ceiling. "Maybe a change of scenery is good for the girls. They're at that age where they're besties one minute and the next they're going after each other like gladiators in the Coliseum. At times I fantasize about sending in the lions." She held out her champagne glass. "Someone top me off with the bubbly, please. One more, and *no*, I'm not driving."

Joan lifted the Champagne bottle from the coffee table and refreshed her drink.

"Should I call the paper and ask them to print a retraction?" I asked.

"No," Esmeralda, Joan, and Cheryl said in unison.

"Then what do I do? They're being assholes."

"They're always assholes," Esmeralda said.

"What do you *want* to do?" Joan asked.

"I wish you wouldn't use the 'A' word in front of my kids," Cheryl said.

"We know what an "asshole" is, mother," Diana yelled down. "It's what you call Papa when you argue."

The door banged open, a chilly wind blasting into the cavernous room. Nick squeezed through the opening, wrestling a large, bulky, green tree behind him. "To the left," he said. "No. A little to the right. Hold on. Lift it up, Cristoph. Not that high up. Wait, wait—" A branch collided with a lamp on the foyer table, and it crashed to the floor.

"Crap!" I said, jumped up, and ran toward it. "What are you doing?"

"Decorating, darling," Nick said. "Christmas is sneaking up on us. The festivities start so early these days. Don't forget we promised Royal Nana a home-cooked meal, a decorated tree, and real eggnog. Did we destroy anything remarkable?"

CHAPTER 5

"Y**ou tell me," I said, gingerly lifting the large shards from the floor and placing them on the side table. "It was the antique Meyda Tiffany glass lamp that your third cousins sent us as a wedding present. But you are in luck my friend, because I am a whiz with super glue."

"Crap!" Prince Cristoph said, popping his head in the room, his blonde hair longish, loose curls caressing the collar of his thick blue fleece jacket. "I'm sorry! What do you want me to do with the fat end of this tree?"

"Hold it still for a moment and don't move, wanker." Nick wiped the sweat from his brow. "It's not a genuine Tiffany, Lucy. It's an expert knock-off. Impossible to tell the difference unless light fixtures are your thing. Besides, Nana never liked that side of the family. She said they were cheapskates and charlatans."

"Oh. But I liked this lamp. It was so pretty."

"I know, darling. I'm sorry. We'll get another."

"No worries. If it makes you feel any better, my entire family couldn't have banded together to buy us this present. It still would have been too pricy." That was because my entire family consisted of my Uncle John and me. He still lived at The Vail Assisted Living Facility on the Southside of Chicago where I continued to pay his rent. Luckily for us, I'd recently scored a new part-time job after I rescued Nick from the horrible Weddings R Us kidnappers.

The Friedricksburg Chamber of Commerce VP of Marketing caught a glimpse of me on TV, thought I was brave and feisty, and believed that Fredonia desperately needed heroes during these troubled times. Especially curvy, girly heroines who could toss their abundant hair, smile convincingly at a camera while flashing their pearly whites, and strike a pose as they guzzled a bottle of Friedricksburg sparkling mineral water in between nibbling on a Friedricksburg Chateux dark chocolate bar.

In this odd turn of events, I became the new spokeswoman for this small hamlet that was the birthplace of Nicholas's father, King Fredrick Timmel. There were even hushed whispers in the frenetic corridors of advertising offices in the capital city of Sauerhausen that I was in the running to become the new poster child for tourism in Fredonia. My new job might have felt daunting, but I was grateful I didn't have to impersonate anyone other than a happy, parched version of myself. "Perhaps, Nicholas, your cousins have just fallen on tough times."

"Perhaps Nicholas just needs to pick up the other end of the tree," Cristoph said. "Only an asshat leaves his brother standing half in and half out of the door during a cold snap."

The scent of fresh pine needles enveloped me as visions of sugarplum fairies danced in my head, or perhaps it was simply sugar cookies—no, make that plums and fairies. "Wait a minute. Oh my God. I just realized. It's our first Christmas tree as a married couple! Hang on. I'll help." I raced from the living room to the foyer. "Tell me what to do."

"No need. We've got it. Right, dude?" Nick asked. "On

the count of three. One. Two..." They pulled and pushed, see-sawing the ten-foot Christmas tree through the door and into our flat. Cristoph collapsed onto his knees and burst out laughing. "You had to get the biggest one in the lot."

"Only the best for my new bride." Nick pulled me flush against him, grabbed me around the waist, and tickled me. I giggled.

"What's so funny, Lucy?"

"You."

"Take me seriously, wife." He pulled me closer, if that were even possible.

"I'll take you seriously when you kiss me seriously." I gazed up into his crystal blue eyes.

"I am so going to kiss you seriously," he said.

"Stop talking about it and do it."

And he did. His lips were cool from winter's frosty air and yet they warmed me in seconds. My Nicholas, my new husband, was hot. So very, very hot. What was I worried about? This ridiculous thing with stupid Archbishop Causes-desperdues, as well as the meanies in the press with their dire headlines proclaiming that we were not married had to be gossip-mongering. Simply a waste of time. A way to peddle lies and poorly written stories. And what was up with that stupid, fake copy of our marriage certificate with "Null" and "Void" stamped all over it? An asshat, a ne'er do well, a prankster most likely sent that to us. But that didn't stop me from wondering why we hadn't yet received definitive confirmation: were we married or not?

"Worry's etched all over your pretty face." Nick smiled down at me. "I love you. Everything's going to be all right."

"I love you too." My heart pitter-pattered and I nestled in against the hardness of Nick's body, like he was bourbon and I was water. Our pairing was totally meant to be: kismet, fate, a dream come true. Soon I'd be spending my first Christmas as a wedded woman with my new husband, the handsomest man on the European continent, in picture perfect Fredonia with a smattering of snowflakes and abundant goodwill toward mankind. Maybe if I was lucky, I'd score a little peace on Earth, and much needed respite from those crazy months of wedding planning and dieting to fit in the damn wedding dress.

"Show me your best, Nicholas." I whispered, and couldn't help but bite my lip in anticipation. "Don't hold back. Give me all my Christmas presents tonight."

"Oh, I won't be holding back, my princess." He smiled, cupped a muscular hand on my ass, pulled me flush against him, and kissed me again, claiming my mouth with his lips and tongue.

"Can we get rid of all these people?" I whispered after I came up for air.

"I doubt it."

"That sucks."

"Enough already with the PDAs," Cristoph said. "We combed Christmas tree lots for hours. We were torn between a long needled pine and a short needle fir. Ladies. I see you are gathered in the living room around a toasty fire, enjoying your bubbly. What do you think about our selection?"

"It's spectacular," Cheryl said.

"Majestic but homey," Joan said.

I reluctantly pulled away from Nick and gazed at the freshly cut long needled pine tree and inhaled. It was fantabulous. I was half tempted to bury my face in the midst of its aromatic, supple needles, and let the scent brush against my skin and mark my blouse. Who needed perfume when you could smell like Christmas? "I can't believe you got it in our front door. It will look perfect next to the fireplace. I just wish I had all my mom's ornaments from Chicago."

"The tree will look awesome adjacent to Royal Nana's housewarming present," Joan said.

"Right," I said and stared up her gift—an oil painting of Her Royal Highness Marie Susannah Clothilde Timmel when she was young, regal, and sported only one chin—not five. Royal Nana stared out from the middle of the painting as determined as she was now when she commanded a room from the center of her walker.

"Cristoph helped. I rang up my no good, lazy sibling, and put him to work," Nick said. "Best part about moving next door to family. Free labor."

"Let's not forget who found you this place," Cristoph said. "I knew my neighbors wanted to sell. A little bird slipped you the info, and you were able to make a presumptive offer on the place. A quick escrow. Very little hassle. You owe me when my new billiard table's delivered."

"Only if you're planning to install it on the first floor," Nick said.

"First floor or third. You made me visit three Christmas tree farms to find the perfect tree for Lucy and your new place. You owe me."

Crown Prince Cristoph of Fredonia was ten months older than Nicholas. He was muscular, chiseled, and a buttery blonde. The brothers' eyes were similar in shape and intensity of gaze: Nick's blue, Cristoph's hazel. Both mesmerizing.

I liked Cristoph. He was a good guy: sexy, handsome, total eye candy. He was a hot mess of ripped muscles, possessing the willful abandon and naughtiness of a puppy. He'd slept with half of the eligible ladies of Europe, a fair share of commoners, and from what I could feel on the few times we bumped up against each other—he was packing a meaty punch under his beltline. Yet I still left him high and dry at the altar because I was completely, unequivocally in love with his younger brother, Nicholas.

Now, Cristoph, the heir to the throne walked toward me, leaned down, and gave me a peck on the cheek. "How's married life, Lucy? Dull, I assume. You're married to my very staid younger brother. If you ever change your mind and remember me fondly, you know where I live. Approximately one hundred twenty five meters to the right."

"I know you think that's funny. But the weird thing is, I'm not sure Nick and I are really married."

"We *are* married!" Nick said. "Lucy's off limits, dude. You had your shot. Good tidings, ladies. My brother, the very eligible playboy prince is in the house. Are any of you single? I'm not sure you were expecting his company. He's quite the ladies man you know. I hope you're all clothed." He unzipped his black fleece jacket, hanging it on a wrought iron hallway hook.

"What does it matter? We're cousins and we've seen each other naked since we were toddlers," Esmeralda said. "Cristoph was the one fascinated with his penis. You, on the other hand were exploring places and things, fantasizing that one day you would conquer the world."

"Or at least the sandbox," Cristoph said.

"Enough talk of existentialism and penises," Cheryl said, wandering past us into the kitchen. "I'm making fresh hot cocoa. There's enough for everyone."

"Penises?" Esmeralda lifted an eyebrow. "My kind of holiday party."

"Dirty girl!" Cheryl said. "I was talking about the cocoa."

"Proud to be a dirty girl," Esmeralda said.

"I've always loved that about you," Cristoph said. "I swear if we weren't cousins, we'd have shagged by now."

"Nice try, opportunist," Esmeralda said. "You're too pretty. Not my type."

"I could totally be your type. Don't forget, cousins married all the time in the olden days."

"The olden days have come and gone." She waved one hand in the air dismissively. "Besides, when have I ever wanted to settle down?"

"Never," Joan said.

"That's right," Esmeralda said. "One lover for the rest of my life equals a coach class ticket to boring."

"I'm first class, darling," Cristoph said. "And no one's ever accused me of being boring."

"Can we move on from the pervy cousin sex talk?" I asked. "I've got a problem. I ordered one thousand mono-grammed, official Royal Fredonia thank you notes on white linen paper. I purchased the 'Fredonia Forever' stamps, and no, the monarchy has not reimbursed me for any of that yet. And—"

"Good luck with that one," Lady Cheryl said. "They turned down my request for tuition compensation for dental assistant school three times."

There was a hesitant knocking on the door. "Expecting more guests?" Nicholas asked.

"No." I made my way to the entrance, peered through the peephole and stared at the guard and a short, white-haired man with a clerical collar poking out from the top of his winter overcoat. "Can I help you Private Parker?"

"A Father Leo Florentine here to see you Ms. Missus."

"I apologize for the intrusion, but it's a bit of an emer-gency," the man said.

"Yes, of course," I said, opening the door. "Hello, Father. How can I help you? Do you need a donation for the Holy Cross Orphanage? Nick! Did we forget to write a holiday check for the orphanage?"

"It's not about the orphanage. You *are* Lucille Marie Trab-bicio?" he asked, his gray eyes peering down at me.

"Yes and no. That would be my official name in my former life before I married the old ball and chain here." I jabbed my thumb in Nick's direction. "Technically, now I'm Mrs. Lucille Timmel."

"We've been trying to reach you by phone, but some rude lady keeps hanging up on us."

"Oh," I said. "Rest assured I'll have a word with her!"

Nick rolled his eyes at me. "I'd like a word with her too. Do come in, Father. "

"Thank you, Your Highness." He scraped his feet on the mat before entering the foyer.

"Call me Nick. Can we get you anything?"

"No thank you. I'm afraid I have bad tidings."

"Bad tidings?" Esmeralda got up and eased toward the door.

"Hopefully they're not *too* bad," Joan said, making her way toward me.

"How bad could it be?" I asked and broke out into a sweat.

Esmeralda whipped a red silk hand fan out of her purse, flipped it open with a brisk *clack*, and waved it in front of my face.

"It seems that the priest who performed your marriage, Father McGillicuddy, wasn't technically licensed to marry you," Father Florentine said.

"Yes, yes. I've already heard that. Apparently there's some kerfuffle about his standing in the Holy Church," I said. "Did Father McGillicuddy screw up on communion? Hand out the wafers before the wine? Is he behind on his re-licensure hours?"

"I wish it were that easy." He sighed, removed his hat, and pressed it over his heart. "Archbishop Causesdesperdues asked me to investigate the issue. At first I thought it was a simple clerical error. But then I dove down a rabbit hole, and discovered a much darker secret."

"Darker?" Nick asked.

"That sounds ominous," Joan said, and placed a reassuring hand on my arm.

"It is," Father Florentine said, and crossed himself. "Father McGillicuddy didn't just screw up your paperwork. It would have been so simple if he didn't dot an i or cross a t. Unfortunately this isn't a simple case of re-sign the documents, send them back in, and get everything stamped for approval. It turns out the man who married you wasn't the *real* Father McGillicuddy. I regret to inform you that you and Prince Nicholas were married by a man *posing* as Father McGillicuddy. You were married by a priest impersonator."

"Uh... Uh," I said, felt my knees go weak, and I clutched the door frame. "What does this mean?"

"This means that you are certainly, completely, one hundred percent not legally married. You, Lucille Marie Trabbicio, were *never* royally wed."

CHAPTER 6

I shoved my hands over my mouth, raced to the bathroom, collapsed on my knees before the porcelain god and threw up for a solid ten minutes. I heard Nick gently scaring everyone out of our townhouse with polite entreaties to visit soon—*very soon*—once we had decorated the tree.

"You're kicking us out at the wrong time, Nicholas," Esmeralda said from beyond the bathroom door. "We ladies can help. We facilitate, finagle. Good times, or bad—we get things done. This is what we do best."

"I know," he said. "But Lucy's my wife—"

"Apparently not," Esmeralda said.

He sighed. "Let me talk with her first and then I'll apprise you of the situation."

"Don't make me wait too long, cousin," she said. "I'm an impatient girl." And the door banged shut.

A half hour later I pushed myself off the cold marble floor of the guest bathroom and gazed up into the gilded mirror. My mascara was running, my complexion was sallow, and I resembled a sad clown wannabe who had auditioned for clown school but in a cruel twist of fate had been rejected for being too on-the-nose. I brushed my teeth, rinsed out my mouth and applied Friedricksburg natural beeswax lip balm—that stuff didn't smudge.

I wandered into our living room. Father Florentine sat on a brown leather side chair, drinking one of Cheryl's mugs of steaming cocoa and stared up at the oil painting of Nick's grandmother. "Her Royal Highness Marie Susannah Clothilde Timmel was a splendid monarch. An amazing ruler," he said. "And quite the looker in her day. In a way I feel I've let her down by delivering this horrible news to you."

"It's not your fault, Father," Nick said, taking a seat on the red velvet couch. He patted the space next to him. I plunked down alongside him and rested my head on his shoulder. He picked up my hand, wove his fingers between mine, and gave them a reassuring squeeze.

"Look. I don't care whose fault this is," I said. "I don't care that Father McGillicuddy was an imposter, or a poser—maybe he had good reason. Perhaps he was protecting a family member, or collecting extra prayers for someone he cared about who was sick. All I want to know is, how do we fix this?"

"Lucy, don't worry about this tonight." Nick raised my hand to his lips and kissed it. "Besides, there's something I need to tell you."

I glared at him. "Of *course* I'm worrying about this tonight. Why put off until tomorrow what you can get done today? What do you need to tell me? I know the Christmas tree needs decorating. I know we owe your grandmother a spectacular home-cooked meal, and I'm woefully behind on thank you notes. But now I'm not even sure I should send them because maybe, *just maybe* I'm supposed to return all the presents because technically we're not married, and some day, someone might accuse us of making out like bandits by keeping presents that weren't rightfully ours because we're," I hiccupped. "Not." I hiccupped again. "Even married!"

Father Florentine crossed himself, and mumbled under his breath in Latin. "The artist's choice of colors on Her Royal Highness's portrait are refreshing. What a splendid opportunity to see them up close." He pushed himself to standing, walked toward the wall next to the fireplace, and gazed up stony-eyed at the grand painting.

"Lucy," Nick said. "I am here at your side. We will figure this out."

"It's too late. I'm a laughingstock." I wrung my hands. "All the gossips and meanies will just eat this story up alive. They'll spoon it down like it's chocolate pudding with a dollop of Cool Whip on top."

"What's Cool Whip?"

"Don't worry about it."

"We will totally figure this out. We will go to the ends of the Earth to find the answer. We will determine the best course of action, right after I finish guard duty."

"I'm sorry. Guard duty?"

Nick stood up. "Kurt, the royal scheduling secretary, reminded me that the palace prefer I finish off my obligatory Fredonia National guard duty before year's end. I could defer my service, but in the wake of our recent weddings, less fortunate Fredonia citizens might perceive that as entitlement. And frankly, I wouldn't blame them. I'll only be gone a short while."

"You're leaving?" I blinked.

"Tomorrow. It's only for a week. Ten days tops. A brief deployment. I know it's shitty news on top of more shitty news. I'm so sorry, my love."

"Where are you going? What are you doing? Oh, Nicholas —is it dangerous?"

"No. It's simple Royal Fredonia Helicopter rescue missions: nothing all that spectacular. I'll bone up on my paramedic and flying skills. Be reminded how to tie some of those knots. Pop over to Italy, France, Spain for a few brief missions. Whatever the military and palace deem appropriate. Then I'll be back here with you to add the finishing decorations to the tree. And if we need to get royally wed again in order to make our marriage official, that's what we'll do."

"You'd royally wed me again?"

"I'll royally wed you as many times as it takes to stick." Nick leaned down, kissed me, then whispered in my ear. "But I won't stop royally bedding you in the meantime..."

"Unfortunately, Your Highness, getting re-married poses a bit of a problem," Father Florentine said, scratching under his clerical collar with one finger. His neck flushed crimson red.

"What's the problem?" Nick asked.

"It's not *my* problem. Or that of the New Reformed Church of Fredonia," he said.

"Whose problem is it?" I asked.

"The older, more traditional Church of Fredonia frowns upon a member of the royal family marrying a person who was previously married."

"But, according to you Nick and I were never wed," I said.

"Oh, but you *were* wed, Ms. Trabbicio. Vows were spoken, paperwork was signed, and the service was officiated by a man whose real name is Milton Mertz, an ordained minister in the Society of Royal Alchemists."

"Alchemists perform weddings?" I asked.

"Yes. They think they can turn anything into gold. If you wanted to roll the dice, I think that the palace and the Reformed Church of Fredonia would turn a benevolent blind eye on the legality of your marriage. But when you have children, should there be a claim to the throne, or a nit-picky bully decide to rise up against you, anyone can find the text in the canons of the Old Church of Fredonia as well as the royal bylaws. Chapter ten, page one hundred and fifteen states..." He pulled out a folded piece of paper from his lapel coat pocket, opened it, and blinked. "I can't believe I forgot my readers."

"Pass it to me, please?" He handed me the note, and I read aloud. "Any woman who has previously engaged in the holy sacrament of matrimony is not eligible to wed a Prince of Fredonia."

"Apologies, Father," Nicholas said. "I'm confused. Might you explain this in greater detail?"

"This tiny rule marks Lucille as being previously married. Anyone who has been previously wed is not eligible to marry a Prince or Princess of Fredonia."

"Wait a minute." I slapped my palm to my forehead and paced back and forth in front of the Christmas tree. "You're saying I was *never* married to Nick but then on the other hand you're saying I *was* married to Nick."

"Exactly."

"My head is rotating faster than a salad spinner."

"What's a salad spinner?" Nick asked.

"Don't worry about it."

"Welcome to bureaucracy and the joys of determining royal rules and protocol," Father Florentine said. "These sticky points can drive one to drink. Not all that fun, is it?"

"This is the craziest thing I've ever heard," I said, my hands shaking, when the large flat screen TV hanging on the wall over the fireplace played a Christmas carol. "Nicholas. Why is our TV playing "Deck the Halls"? I know it's the holidays and that I need to get around to decking our halls, but right now I'm not sure I can handle one more pinch of pressure."

"I hooked it up to get Facetime calls." Nick picked up the remote and aimed it at the seventy-inch flatscreen. "I thought I'd surprise you with our new holiday ringtone." The screen appeared grayish black, morphed to a pixelated blue, and then crystallized into a clear image of Royal Nana. She sat in profile to us, slumped in a comfy blue wingback chair in her condo filled with Christmas Hummel figurines on the coffee table and the fireplace mantel. Her chin rested on her chest, gentle snores emanating from her mouth, slightly ajar.

Lady Esmeralda stood at her side and peered at us through the screen. "Lucy? Nick?"

"Yes," we said.

"She was wide awake fifteen seconds ago, when I hit send. Nana, wake up!" Esmeralda massaged her shoulders and Her Highness stirred.

"I can tell from your firm grip, Heinrich my darling, that you're a heap of muscular hunkiness, but I'm not up for sexy times tonight. Check back in with me in the morning."

"*Not* Grandpapa. I'm your grand-niece, Esmeralda."

"You could go places with those hands, young lady," Royal Nana said. "You get that from my side of the family you know."

"Nana, turn and look into the phone. Nicholas and Lucy want to see your face."

"I thought we were calling them," she said. "Why am I supposed to look into the phone?"

"We *are* calling them," Esmeralda said. "The new phones work differently than the old ones."

"Can they still hear us?" She shifted awkwardly in our direction.

"Yes, we can hear you Nana," Nick said. "This is kind of a tricky time. What's up?"

She stared into the screen, her eyes taking on a strange intensity. "What's up is that Esmeralda told me that no good

Archbishop Causesdesperdues sent his lackey Florentine to deliver bad news smack dab in the middle of the holiday season. According to him you're not 'really' married. This does not please me for any number of reasons including that I bought you a 'couples' present. It's personalized and I can't take it back."

"I'm sorry Your Royal Highness." The priest bowed to the TV.

"You don't need to worry about getting a present for me," I said.

"I will not settle for this archaic mumbo-jumbo, Florentine." Nana shook her arthritic finger at him. "I know the twisted spider web of political and religious lies better than most of you. If you think I'm going to sit around and watch my favorite new couple get dicked around by bureaucracy and tangled in fine print, you've got another thing coming."

"I couldn't agree with you more," the priest said.

"Good. Can we change these antiquated laws?"

"That would take years and be very difficult, Your Highness."

"What's *less* difficult?"

"Tracking down the imposter priest and getting a signed affidavit from him that he is not licensed to perform wedding ceremonies," Florentine said.

"But what if he *is* licensed to perform wedding ceremonies?" I asked.

"Then you need to find a loophole," Royal Nana said.

"What kind of loophole?"

"The kind that works. Father Florentine, do you have any idea where this rogue imposter currently lays his conniving head at night?"

"My sources last spotted him in Venice, Italy. He's visiting his brother."

"Do you have an address?"

"Yes."

"Good. I'll need that. Lucy and Nick—pack your overnight bags—"

"He can't," I said. "Nick has guard duty. It's his job. His royal duty."

Nick shook his head. "I think it's best that I defer—"

"No," I said. "Get it done, Nicholas. That's how we roll."

"I agree with Lucy," Royal Nana said. "It might be rotten timing but your service is necessary. Esmeralda?"

"Yes, Nana."

"Gather the ladies. I'll have my private jet ready to go at 0700 hours."

"Ahem." Herr Fingerlachen interrupted, looming over her shoulder. "Not tomorrow, Your Highness. We took the jet in for servicing."

"We did?"

"That time of the year."

"When do we get it back?"

"Two days." He stared into the phone and waved at us. "Good tidings, Your Highnesses!"

"Just call me Nick, Herr Fingerlachen."

I sighed. "I'm not a Highness."

"Fine. Nick goes to guard duty. Esmeralda gathers the ladies. Fingerlachen will have the jet ready to go at 0700 hours two days from now. That will give me time to arrange for your accommodations and conduct more surveillance on this priest imposter. You'll fly to Venice, track him down, and handle this situation before the press definitively confirms the marriage is off."

"What do you mean by *'handled'*?" Esmeralda asked.

"I want Lucy and Nicholas unwed, or even better *never wed* by this charlatan. After that we will quickly and quietly get them married *for good* this time by an official member of the clergy who is accepted by the palace as well as the Royal

Church of Fredonia, both old and new versions. I'm an old lady, I need a little Christmas cheer, and this will not be the coal in my stocking. I expect this kerfuffle to be settled before Christmas, or I will not be happy. And when I'm very unhappy—heads roll."

CHAPTER 7

I stayed up half the night having hot going-away sex with my beloved Nicholas. The next morning I poured two mugs of the extra strong coffee in our kitchen, dressed in my warm, striped pink flannel onesie pajamas with the feet. I handed Nick a cup, grabbed a kitchen towel, and wiped down a small spill on the counter. "Promise me that you'll be careful."

"You be careful," he said. "I'm not thrilled you're doing this without me. I'd send Cristoph with you, but Nana said that would just call more attention. Don't forget he's on call if you need anything."

"He's baby-sitting Tulip." I glanced over at our dog sprawled out on the foyer rug, wagging her tail upon hearing her name.

"My mom can do that. I love you so very much, Lucy." He kissed me on the lips and sighed. "Why does our relationship have to be so complicated?"

"Has it ever been simple?"

He cracked a smile. "Hah! And yet we fell in love anyhow.

I fear you're stuck with me." He set his cup on the counter, turned, and walked toward his coat on the wall peg.

He looked adorable in his uniform. Those khaki pants hugged his tight ass. I simply couldn't resist, and towel slapped him. "No—you're stuck with *me*."

"Hey! I beg to differ." He turned and swooped me up in his muscular arms, tickling my waist, and blowing kisses onto my neck.

"Stop." I giggled. "You've got to get out of here."

But he carried me to the pudding couch, and tossed me on top. "You look like a bunny in those pajamas." He joined me on the sofa, straddling me, a rakish smile growing on his lips. He reached for the zipper at the top of my onesie and inched it down, slipping his hand under the warm fleece, caressing my neck, my collarbone, circling down and grazing my breast, skimming my waist. "You know what bunnies are notorious for, yes?"

I inhaled sharply and lied. "I have no idea."

"Then I'll have to remind you," he said, and proceeded to do just that.

A half hour later I stood in the foyer, zipped up my onesie, and dragged a hand through my hair that felt like the aforementioned bunnies had nested in it. "You're going to be late, Nicholas. And then they'll dock you and make you scrub the decks or something."

"It's always something." He snagged his warm military-styled woolen jacket off the peg on the foyer wall, shrugged it on, and reached into the pocket. "That reminds me. I want you to have this before Christmas." He pulled out a black velvet jewelry box and extended it toward me.

Color me intrigued.

"No." I shook my head. "Let's do the gift giving thing when you get back."

"This isn't your Christmas present. It's something I've

been holding onto. I've wanted to give it to you for a while now, and with our shitty news, I don't know, this just feels like the right time. Come on. Open it."

I took the black box from him, cracked open the top, my eyes widening.

A lustrous antique gold ring nestled inside the box. Its setting was narrow in the back and grew chunkier along the top where the bezels circled a round center stone that was probably a four carat diamond. "Holy smokes. It's gorgeous." I glanced at my significant finger on my left hand. Yup, my pretty engagement ring with the diamonds and rubies was still there. "But where..."

"You can size it for any finger you want, or put it on a chain and make it into a necklace. It was my great grand-mother's. Cristoph might inherit the throne but I get more than my share of the good family jewelry." He took it from me, poised to slip it on the fourth finger of my right hand, but I shook my head.

"Do that when you come back to me."

He tucked it back in the box, leaned down, and kissed the top of my head. "I love you, Lucy. Be safe while I'm gone. Promise me you'll be careful on this, your newest adventure. Look me in the eyes and promise me."

"I promise. Now go! Get out of here before you get in trouble."

I kept a stiff upper lip until the gate slammed shut in the front yard of our townhouse. And I sat down on the kitchen floor, my back to the fancy cabinets, hugged my shoulders, and cried.

Two days later Esmeralda, Joan, and Mr. Philips and I flew to Venice in Royal Nana's cushy Gulfstream private jet and landed at Marco Polo Airport's new wing, built to accommodate international flights. After we cleared customs, a porter collected our luggage, placed our bags on a cart, and ferried them down to the facility's adjoining waterside dock.

I needed to think. Exercise always cleared my mental cobwebs, and I refused to be schlepped along with the luggage. We walked the distance from Customs and Immigration to the boat dock.

Now I stood, finding my balance in the polished cedar paneled water taxi as choppy waters slapped against the sides of the vessel. The chilly December wind picked up, and I pulled the sash of my cashmere coat tighter, adjusted my warm lambs wool scarf higher on my neck, and looked back at the airport behind us. "Royal Nana's jet is styling. Like— who has memory foam padded leather seats that recline to a complete horizontal position? I'm starting to think that everything she does is amaze-balls. Our flight was quick. It's the first time I've flown over the Alps and didn't feel like puking. Color me grateful."

"Perhaps this bodes well for our mission," Mr. Philip Philips said, smoothing one sleek black leather gloved clad hand over his immaculate white hair as he gingerly took a seat under a boat tarp that deflected the crisp wind.

Mr. Philips was my former employer but was now practically a father figure to me. Albeit a snotty, meticulous, demanding father figure.

"This trip is spur of the moment. Lady Cheryl flew out yesterday to Crete for the holidays and I'm grateful you could fill in, be on our team, Mr. Philips," I said. "How's your back?"

"Tentative."

"Still doing your stretches and strengtheners?"

"Funny, you don't look like my physical therapist."

"I'm just the girl you walked down the aisle a few weeks ago during my last marriage ceremony. In spite of your fussy grooming habits and persnickety ways, I like you. That said, I counted on you to be my lucky charm, and assumed that particular wedding was a keeper. Was your mojo off that day?"

"Don't blame me for your recent bad luck in the matrimonial department," he said. "I'm still on your team, Lucille. I've been hired to help you and the ladies track down the poser priest, and solve your latest debacle."

"I can live with that. Father McGillicuddy seemed so nice; a dog loving, kind-hearted man of the cloth. Was there something glaringly obvious about his demeanor that I missed? Did I read him wrong?"

He shook his head. "I don't think so. This one just came out of left field. Buck up, we'll figure it out."

"Lucy, have you ever been to Venice before?" Joan asked.

"Yes. I visited with Nick in September for the Venice Carnival Masquerade Ball." I closed my eyes, inhaled the salty air spiked with the scent of jet fuel and fish. It was a far cry from the dimly lit deserted corridor at the Palazzo Delacroix in Venice that smelled of exotic perfumes and sandalwood incense, Puccini playing in the background as peals of laughter from masked partygoers echoed off the walls around us. Hot memories of the naughty things Nick and I had done on a settee in a dark corner of that corridor flooded my brain.

"Fun! Did you see the sights?" Joan asked as she peered down at us from the platform leading to the boat, one designer clad foot resting on the first rung of the stepladder.

"Hmm, let me think. *The sights...*"

Nick's lips sliding down my cleavage. His fingers impatiently unlacing and tugging my low cut lace corset as I halfheartedly tried to push his hands away. "Stop, bad boy! We're going to get caught."

"We've never gotten caught before." His two-day scruff of a beard scraped against the smooth, sensitive skin of my breast.

"Yes, we have. Don't you remember that trip to the Guggenheim..." His tongue circled one nipple, his teeth nipping as zippy, yummy sensations flooded my body making their way to my brain—like I'd downed two mugs of steaming hot chocolate on a cold winter day.

"Which trip to the Guggenheim?" He came up for air, glanced up and smiled, but then drew my breast back into his mouth, hungry.

"What's a Guggenheim?" I asked, twisting my fingers through his long black hair, pulling him closer to me.

"I saw more than my fair share of sights, Joan." I sighed. "All were lovely, thank you."

The water taxi's driver hoisted our bags into the boat. Per Nana's advice, I had packed a small overnighter. Mr. Philips traveled with his neat, compact bag and his man purse slung crosswise over his shoulder. Apparently Joan hadn't gotten the memo and had brought one very large French designer wheeled suitcase that would have been too big to carry on a commercial flight.

Esmeralda probably *did* get the memo but didn't care as she toured with two bags: an overnighter and a trunk that was roomy enough to transport a dead body. A chill swept over me and I suddenly hoped our mission wouldn't come to that.

Joan hesitated on the ladder, glancing down at me.

I held out my hand to her. "Come on, get in. What's wrong? Are you scared of water?"

"Of course not. You shouldn't listen to those rumors. I think I strained a glute muscle." She rubbed her right cheek with the heel of her hand. "I jumped a foot when the Customs Officer pinched my ass."

"If you pulled a butt muscle from getting squeezed by that tiny man with the impish smile, you need to get out of your office, get pinched more frequently, and build up tolerance," Esmeralda said, also holding out one gloved hand to her.

"Americans call that sexual harassment, you know," Joan said as we helped her into the water taxi. She stumbled, nearly toppling Esmeralda, but I grabbed onto her and together we managed to right each other.

"Italians call that life," Esmeralda said as we took our seats on the boat's perimeter.

"Buon Giorno bella signore." The driver backed the boat out of the slip, and taxied out of the harbor into the choppier waters of the Adriatic Sea. "E' un viaggio d' affair o di piacere?"

"Entrambi," Esmeralda said.

"What did he say?" I asked.

"He wanted to know if we were visiting for business or pleasure. She told him both." Joan tugged her scarf higher on her neck. "It's awfully chilly on the Adriatic this time of year. Why didn't we take a car?"

"Because we always take cars," Esmeralda said. "The winds might be brisk, but journeying by boat to Venice is so much more fun. Think of it as an adventure."

"It would be if the cold, wet air wasn't seeping into my bones." Mr. Philips shivered.

"Thank your lucky stars your bones still feel something," Esmeralda said. "That means you're alive and kicking. Considering your complexion is opalescent on a good day—I was beginning to wonder. Why don't you take a seat inside the cabin? It will be warmer."

"But then I won't have the best views of our arrival into bella Venezia."

"You can't have everything," Joan said. "I learned that one a long time ago."

"Right." He sighed, stood up, and lurched down the steps into the boat's interior. "I'm pouring myself a Bellini. Join me should your bones need warming."

☙❧

An hour later, my ladies had abandoned me for the warmth of the boat's cabin and Mr. Philips' Champagne cocktails. Besides the driver, I was the only person still on top of the vessel, tucked into the hug of a red leather seat, hands jammed in my pockets. I shivered, not knowing if it was from the cold or the gorgeous sights of this magical city as we churned through the waters of the Grand Canal.

Renaissance, Classic, and Baroque-styled buildings four to eight stories tall lined the waterway, adjoining docks leading to them with all kinds and sizes of boats secured to their piers. Clunky, modern waterbuses, water taxis, and quaint old-fashioned gondolas occupied with tourists snapping pics with their smart phones motored past us in both directions.

I recognized the San Marco Princessa Palazzo—our five star home away from home—in the near distance from checking out its website the day before. The eight-story hotel was a washed out pink and appeared more weathered in real life than on the Internet: almost as if the facility had slipped in status, delicately dropping half a star. But as Royal Nana had once told me, age snuck up on the best of us, and thankfully beauty was in the eye of the beholder.

Our driver throttled down and maneuvered the sleek, vintage vessel toward the hotel's dock. The Princessa had been Royal Nana's first pick of accommodations. Through the mist of wintery weather, the grand dame appeared, slightly worn around the edges, albeit not quite as much as Nick's grandmother. Its tiny balconies were framed by shutters, and barnacle shells clung to the wood pilings that made up its dock.

The driver turned off the boat's engine, jumped onto the bow and scrambled with ropes to secure the vessel to the landing. "Benvenuti a San Marco Princessa Palazzo!" He hopped onto the pier and extended his hand to me.

"Thank you." I held onto his calloused palm and took that big, first step from the boat onto the weathered planks.

Mr. Philips exited the cabin, climbed onto the dock, and paid the captain, who promptly jumped back in the vessel, and passed our suitcases up to a hotel bellman. Esmeralda accepted the help of a middle-aged concierge and climbed from the boat onto the dock. "Grazie mille."

Joan stared at the pier from the inside of the boat, her knees knocking. "Hello! Could someone give me a little help, please?"

The bellman paused, then leaned down and held out his hand.

"I don't know why this makes me so nervous," she said, taking it. "It's just a little water. What's there to be scared of other than falling under the boat, knocking one's head, and nearly drowning because no one saw you go under?"

She stepped onto the dock and stared down, as if landing here had been questionable. "Thank you," she said.

"You are beautiful," he said in Italian.

"You are too kind." She blushed.

"Your skin is so white. Your hair so red."

"My name's Lady Joan Brady. What's your name?"

"Whatever you desire it to be, bellissima."

"Oh." She stared at her feet. "Oh."

I gazed up at our new digs, and bit my lip. Here we were in gorgeous Venice, home to artists and celebrities, architects, and scoundrels. It dawned on me that this was the perfect city for a priest impersonator to hide. I was a girl who desperately needed to get royally unwed before I could legally get royally wed. Milton Mertz, priest impersonator, could reinvent himself as anybody doing almost anything here. How in the heck could we track him down, let alone coerce him to sign the affidavit that Royal Nana insisted that I wrangle from him?

Suddenly I felt defeated before we'd even begun to fight. Like I'd given blood twice in the same day, or someone had let all the air out of my tires. I wasn't a wuss: I'd experienced my fair share of hard times, the worst being losing both my parents in a motorcycle crash. Getting over that had not been a walk in the park. I'd worked a wide variety of menial and difficult part-time jobs. I'd endured more than my fair share of being demeaned, belittled, and undermined, let alone under-estimated.

I gazed at my ladies. They were so fashionable, fierce, and formidable. This blanket statement included Mr. Philips—whether he liked me calling him a lady or not—I didn't really care at this point. I had friends, excellent backup, and our common denominator was that none of us were fond of taking prisoners.

I reminded myself that not only was I a Chicago girl, I was also part Italian. I vowed on my parents' graves to track down this priest impersonator. I would bring him to justice, and find my loophole, as Royal Nana had insisted, if it was the last thing I ever did.

CHAPTER 8

"Y ou've got this odd look on your face. Like you ate bad sushi or something. What are you thinking?" Esmeralda asked as we walked toward the palazzo's entrance. Evergreen garlands covered in twinkling holiday lights draped over the archways above the doors, hand blown Murano Christmas glass ornaments dangled from them accentuating the prettiness of the Princessa's entrance.

"Besides the obvious? I can't help but wonder what Venice has in store for me this trip. Nick's not here, so there won't be any romance."

"Speak for yourself," Esmeralda said.

"I'm taking Lucy's share of the romance on this trip," Joan said, trailing on our heels. "My ass just got pinched again. I think it was the captain. Or the bellboy. It all happened so fast."

"I hope it was your other cheek," I said. "Otherwise you'll bruise. I've got Rescue Remedy in my suitcase. Remind me when we get to our room."

"*Suite*," Mr. Philips said. "We're not staying at the Jolly Rancher Motel and we're not dallying. This isn't va-cay, ladies.

We're checking in, changing clothes, and getting down to business."

Esmeralda saluted him. "You run a tight ship, Captain Philips. Maybe Tom Hanks would play you in the movie adaptation."

"I don't have a problem with that," he said. "I'm not here to hold your hands, buy you 'I Heart Venice' trinkets, or take selfies with you as we feed the pigeons in the Piazza San Marco. Her Royal Highness Marie Susannah hired me to track down this slippery priest imposter, and ensure Lucille Trabbicio is one hundred percent, royally unwed at the end of this operation."

"Got it. I buy my own trinkets," Esmeralda said. "Does this assignment have a code name?"

"Mission Venice," Mr. Philips said.

"That's boring," Esmeralda said.

"Practical's a better word," Mr. Philips said.

"What about Mission Serenissima?" Joan asked. "After all, the city of Venice is nicknamed Serenissima."

"I could go for a little 'serene' right about now." I gazed at a line of tired tourists at the front desk in the hotel lobby and stopped in my tracks. Not to be bitchy, but the last thing I wanted to do right now was stand in line. I'd been standing in line to get married and frankly, I was starting to feel like I'd been standing in line to live my life.

"Follow me." The concierge in the gray suit waved his hand in the air. "You've already been checked in."

"Disaster averted," Esmeralda said, as we gratefully bypassed the tired-looking queue.

"It's the power of the correct code name," Joan whispered. "Serenissima."

"I love it, Joan. No matter what craziness transpires—we will be unhurried, unworried, and serene. And we will dally if we want to dally."

"No you won't," Mr. Philips frowned. "You can take all the time in the world when you're a tourist. You already dallied in the hallways of Palazzo Delacroix during a Masquerade ball because you didn't think you'd ever be caught. But trust me, eventually you will be caught, and there will be consequences."

"What are you talking about?" I asked.

Mr. Philips sighed, unbuckled his man purse, removed a manila envelope, and handed it to me. "Palace Internet monitors discovered these images for sale on line. We bought them from a rascal named 'Steve' from Downers Grove, Illinois, who also attended the Venice Masquerade ball in September."

I flipped through the array of photos of me and Nick and heatedly making out in the darkened corridor at the Delacroix Palazzo, and all the little hairs on my arms stood up. "Wowsa!" Nicholas looked so freaking hot, his dark hair tumbling into his face, his hand kneading my breast.

"Wowsa, indeed," Mr. Philips said. "We told Steve that his photos were fuzzy, we weren't convinced the half-naked couple in the picture was Prince Nicholas of Fredonia and his adorable fiancé' Lucy Trabbicio, the future princess. And yet we still wished to purchase them from him and take them off the market for a reasonable price."

"I'm sorry we put the palace through more trouble." I was embarrassed, not only for the obvious reasons, but also because the longer I gazed at the photos it was obvious I'd waited too long too get my highlights touched up.

"Maybe you two lovebirds need to stop throwing caution to the wind and be a little more careful about where and when you engage in your trysts," Mr. Philips said.

"Maybe you're a big, old wet blanket."

"Maybe you and Prince Nicholas are playing with fire."

"Maybe we like to roast marshmallows on sticks over a bonfire."

"Maybe I'll light your hair on fire if you and Nick don't calm down on the PDAs."

"You wouldn't do that, Philips. Underneath your gruff exterior, you're a softie. I know exactly who you are and what makes you tick."

"If you hear ticking, Lucille, at this point I'd assume it's a bomb. Don't take this lightly."

❧

We followed the Princessa's middle-aged concierge with his thick salt and pepper hair and dressed in an impeccable black, shiny suit, down a thickly-carpeted hallway with framed oil paintings of Rembrandt, Bellini, and Picasso on the walls. He pushed the call button on an old-fashioned elevator, as tiny lights above it illuminated each numbered floor. The lift finally pinged to a stop in front of us. He pulled back the black metal grate, bowed slightly, and gestured to the cage's interior. "Signore e Signori."

We entered the small, elegantly-appointed lift decorated with pristine, gilded wallpaper. The concierge pressed the button for the penthouse. The elevator paused, then groaned, its gears working, as we rose toward the top floor, where it arrived with a shudder. He held the gate open as we exited.

He took the lead and we followed him down a thickly-carpeted corridor, the bellboy trailing behind us, pushing a cart piled high with our luggage. The doors dotting this hallway were not marked with numbers, instead every third door had a name. The Michelangelo. The Rialto. The Calatrava. The Scalzi. And at last, The Puccini.

"Her Royal Highness Marie Susannah Clothilde Timmel

of Fredonia personally requested that you be housed in the Puccini suite." He paused, stuck the key card in the lock's slot, waited for the 'click' and pushed the door open, waving us through. "She has fond memories of staying here sixty years ago with her husband, Prince Heinrich of Fredonia, on their honeymoon. The Princessa even has a few original photos of them in our memory book."

"Get out of town!" I said. "I would love to see that."

He bowed to me. "That can be arranged, Duchess."

Mr. Philips frowned. "Unfortunately that's why we're here. She's not a Duch—"

"She's not Dutch." Joan glared daggers at him. "Lucy's Easy-Peasy Fresh and Breezy DNA lab results confirm she's Italian, French, German, 13% Irish, a pound of Brit, someone ran through Russia dropping their pants, and can you believe it, she's a pinch of Polynesian."

"OMG! That's fabulous," I said, staring at her. "How do you know this?"

"Remember that time I asked you to spit into the test tube?"

"I thought we were helping one of Cheryl's kids with a school science project."

"We were," Esmeralda said. "We were also examining your DNA."

"Why?"

"We'd started a secret Pinterest board for your and Nick's future children," Joan said.

"We thought your DNA results might help us better visualize what they'd look like." Esmeralda said.

"You know," Joan added, "Find better pics to pin on the secret board. We're visual creatures after all."

"Our future children have a Pinterest board? You've totally been holding out on me!"

"Yes," Joan said. "Friends do that. We'll tell you all about it later—over cocktails."

"Good god. This is so exciting!" I walked around the suite, suddenly invigorated. We were on the top floor of the Princessa Palazzo. The ceilings were tall and arched, a mural with angels and half naked people painted high above us. I took in their cavorting—no judgment—and doubted they'd be all that critical that Nick and I had fooled around in a public corridor at a masked ball.

The bellboy carried our luggage into the three bedrooms, in between his furtive puppy-eyed glances at Joan. "Bellissima," he whispered.

"Stop!" she said.

"This place is amazing." I strode to the main window that opened onto the balcony and took in the view of the Grand Canal. I saw St. Mark's on the right, but my eye was drawn to a small, weathered motorboat in the near distance, its engine idling. A tall man, wearing a long raincoat and hat stood in the boat, peering up at the Princessa Palazzo Hotel through binoculars. His focus flitted between windows until he focused right on me.

I jumped.

He jumped. His boat rocked, and he plunked back down on its simple seat, pulling his hat lower on his forehead.

Who was he? Why was he sitting in his boat, braving the cold breeze in the middle of Venice's Grand Canal staring up at our hotel? "Hey, can someone check out this guy in the boat outside our window?" I pointed with one hand, dug through my purse with the other, searching for my phone.

"No can do honey," Joan said. "Too many handsome men in Venice to check out. Besides, I'm famished. Where can we grab a quick lunch—good food, nothing fancy?"

I aimed my phone at the man through the window, but his back was now toward me as his small boat puttered away.

Strangely, I noticed a black Labrador retriever staring back at me from the vessel. "Hey, does anyone else see the dog in that boat?"

"Trattoria Positano is in walking distance," the concierge said. "Might I assist you with anything else?"

"We're good," Mr. Philips said. He eased down onto the floor in stages, and sighed.

"Philips, you okay?" I asked.

"Fine." He lay on his back, brought his knees in close to his chest, and gave them a squeeze.

"Just so you know," the concierge said. "The hotel windows have a protective reflective covering that deflect paparazzi cameras. That is, unless you open them. Unfortunately, we can't protect the air. As always, Mr. Philips, just pick up the phone or text us, and we will be at your disposal."

"Grazie, Giovanni."

"Anything for you, Philips." The concierge winked at him and left.

გჯე

The concierge was true to his word and dropped off an old scrapbook of Princessa memorabilia. I flipped through its pages and found Royal Nana's honeymoon pictures in Venice from sixty years ago. I perused photos of her and Heinrich, both young and beautiful, standing on their balcony of our very own Puccini suite, overlooking the Grand Canal, staring love struck into each other's eyes.

I couldn't help but think of me and Nicholas. Right now we should be enjoying the beginnings of married life. We should be decorating our tree, fussing with a lamb roast, or a turkey dinner with all the fixings for Royal Nana. Or planning a cocktail party for a few of our friends at the new townhouse overlooking Centralaski Park.

But no.

I couldn't be with my Nicholas. He was somewhere—I didn't know where— stationed on Fredonia National guard duty. Doing manly things in uniform with helicopters, and rescue missions. Dear God, he looked so hot in a uniform. I probably would have fucked him if I was a 1950's housewife in central Illinois and he showed up on my door delivering the milk. 'Yes, Mr. Milkman, I'd love two quarts of the non-homogenized full fat milk to go with your extra serving of pleasuring me sinfully on my kitchen table. Thank you!'

I gave my brain a shake. Back to present, Lucy! I was here in Venice with my Ladies-in-Waiting, and Mr. Philips ready to reclaim my marriage eligibility. I couldn't wait to track down Father McGillicuddy or Milton Mertz—whatever the poser's name was—wrangle a confession out of him and find my loophole. I stared at Mr. Philips lying on the cushy carpeting of our suite, one leg high in the air, his arms clasped around it as he gingerly stretched his hamstring muscles. "Do you need an ice pack, Mr. Philips? A Percocet? Do you want to rest and we'll come back for you?"

"No, Lucille."

"Then chop chop. No dallying, dude. Joan, did you tip the bellboy?"

"Oh, trust me, I'm tipping the bellboy." She slipped the twenty-something besotted young man with the full lips and the black hair her card.

"Let's get a move on. I need to get my life back. But first..." I dug through my bag, and handed Joan my tube of homeopathic anti-bruising ointment. "Slap some of that on your tuches where you were pinched. What's next on the agenda?"

Joan flipped the cap up, squeezed gel on her fingers, and slipped her hand down the back of her pants. "Lunch."

"Shopping," Esmeralda said.

"No. We're on Mission Serenissima," I said. "This trip isn't va-cay."

"Then what are we shopping for?" Joan asked.

"Ball gowns," Mr. Philips said and rolled onto his side, pushing himself up to his knees. "Very high end, expensive ball gowns."

CHAPTER 9

We climbed out of a small water taxi from the canal onto a narrow dock covered in glass shards. I stared up at a graffiti-covered building, and spotted a rat racing yards away from us, scurrying down into the canal. "This doesn't look like the best neighborhood in the world. I'm not a wuss, but maybe we should be shopping in a better zip code."

"We're not here for the ambience, we're here for the dresses," Mr. Philips said.

"Got it." I kicked away a few soggy fliers that clung to my shoe. "Lucky for you all, I took a self-defense course a few years ago."

"Did you learn Krav Maga?" Joan asked.

"Nah. Self-Defense 101 at a community college. We watched *The Karate Kid* and then copied the 'Wax on and Wax off' moves for the rest of the afternoon."

"I feel safer already, Miyagi," Esmeralda said. "I already have a ball gown. I always pack one. You never know when it's going to come in handy."

"Oh, please," Joan said. "The next thing you'll be telling

me is that I need to stuff a scuba mask and snorkel in my bag every time I travel."

"I told you that ten years ago after we did the sneak trip to the Caymans," Esmeralda said. "*And* last year when we spontaneously detoured to Turks and Caicos."

"Fine," she grumbled. "Why are there so many broken bottles down here? Glass shards everywhere. It's downright dangerous. Where have you taken us, Esmeralda?"

"I too have a ball gown. I got it at Nordies Rack in Chicago at a clearance sale. It's my go to dress for fancy events," I said. "But sadly it's stuffed in the back of the townhouse closet."

"Stop debating, ladies. The ball gown shopping is necessary for your next mission that commences tomorrow tonight." Mr. Philips rang the bell of a varnished black door on a four story, narrow, building that appeared like it might crumble into the adjacent canal sometime soon.

"Which is what?" I asked, glancing around at this funky part of town, that no, for once, I hadn't gotten lost in. We had deliberately traveled here to broken glass, smelly fish canal, and graffiti central.

"The opera," Esmeralda said. "We're hitting Teatro La Fenice di Venezia. *Amahl and the Night Visitors* is playing, just for a few nights, in honor of its composer, Gian Carlo Menotti."

"Ooh," Joan said. "My grandmother was in the audience at Rockefeller Center in New York in 1951 when *Amahl and the Night Visitors* played for The Hallmark Channel. I checked out this performance on line months ago but the tickets were already sold out."

"Duchess Edith of Friedricksburg, is a platinum-level patron of the opera house," Esmeralda said. "Royal Nana called in a favor and compliments of her frenemy, we'll be occupying her booth tomorrow night."

"I love that we're taking in a bit of Venice culture, and going to the opera, but honestly, the only thing I want to be doing is tracking down the poser," I said. "This opera thing feels like we're dallying."

"We're not," Esmeralda said. "Based on Royal Nana's investigations, Milton Mertz's half brother is Andrea Mertzolio, the tenor who is admired, but unfortunately, not on anyone's radar. But, that could change after tonight. Andrea's singing the role of one of the kings—a decided bump up from his usual parts."

"Milton and his brother are very close," Mr. Philips said. "He'll probably be in the audience cheering him on. If we're lucky, we can apprehend him at the opera, coerce him to confess, sign a statement and Mission Serenissma will be over and complete."

"I'll be free to marry Nicholas."

"That you will." He pressed his hand on the doorbell again, and glanced at Esmeralda. "I thought you said Gareth Trent was expecting us?"

"He sleeps late."

"It's 2 pm."

"He's an artist. That's like 6 am our time." Esmeralda took a few steps back and gazed up at the shuttered window two stories above the front door. She leaned back, cupping her hands to her mouth. "Get your lazy ass out of bed, Gareth! I've come to collect the ball gowns you promised, and my black Moroccan leather tote. I want it all now."

"Come back later." A rough man's voice called out with a clipped English accent.

"No!"

A Champagne bottle flew out the window aimed straight at my head. I ducked and it shattered onto the small patch of pavement behind me.

"Jeez." Joan hugged her warm coat closer.

I leaned down and dusted a few shards off my leather boots. "I think that explains the broken glass."

"Hold on," the same voice said. Thirty seconds later, the front door creaked open, as Joan and I stared at each other, our eyes widening.

A large hand gestured us inside. "Enter."

"At last, Gareth." Esmeralda took the lead and stomped inside, Mr. Philips on her heels.

"What do you think?" I asked Joan.

"I love his purses. Perhaps we should toast. Lady Cheryl loaned me her Prince Harry's silver flask for good luck." Joan pulled it from her coat pocket, took a slug, and handed it to me. "To procuring beautiful gowns, finding your priest poser, and tracking down your loophole."

I hesitated. "Is it too early in the day to be drinking Scotch?"

Esmeralda leaned out the door, snatched the flask from my hand, and slugged back a shot. "It's after 2 pm. What's wrong with you, Lucy? Hurry up. Gareth's creative window is open, the clock is ticking, and we don't want to miss our opportunity."

I eyed Joan. "What's a creative window?"

She shrugged. "I've never met Gareth Trent. He's probably a precious creative type. Mercurial, genius, a little dotty."

I nodded. "Let's just get this done. Then we can go back to the Princessa and take a nap, or get a massage. Maybe I can try and text Nick, even though I don't think it will go through. Right now I'm feeling a little wound for sound. I need to chill out—"

A half-naked, buff, heavily tatted man with wild salt and pepper hair wearing black pants, leaned out the door and eyed us, smiling through bleary blue eyes. "We'll definitely chill, ladies. Move your hot asses inside my hovel. Especially you." He arched his eyebrows. "The redhead. Let's get this party started."

⚅

We sat on velvet beanbag chairs in Gareth's studio, surrounded by racks filled with ball gowns resembling exotic birds. The smell of medicinal weed wafted through the air as a few young assistants helped us with gowns and purses, and one wizened man served us tiny cups of espresso and an assortment of Italian pastries from an ornate silver tray.

"Joan Brady," Gareth said. "Stop hiding. You're wearing a Gareth Trent original and I will not allow you to wear it like a frightened child."

"I'm not hiding." Joan stared at her feet as she walked across his studio wearing an emerald green three-quarter sleeved long, silk gown with a full skirt and a V neckline. Cinched at the waist, it made her red hair pop and her white complexion glow.

"You walk like you're single at the secondary school dance."

"Don't be mean," I said, munching on a little cake, brushing crumbs from my mouth.

"It's true," he said. "The essence of Joan is sassy, fetching, whatever the hell she wants to be. She just doesn't know it yet."

"Don't worry about it, Lucy," Joan said. "We're here to procure gowns. Not raise our self-esteem."

"That doesn't mean we lose our self respect and dignity in the process."

"She's right," Gareth said. "I'm an asshat. Congratulations Lucky, you called me on it."

"My name's Lucy."

"Joan Brady, I apologize," he said. "Let's try this again. When you walk, lift your head. Don't look at your feet. Let the dress swish around your ankles. As for you, Lucky...I see you in a rose silk dress with a plunging neckline and a nipped in waist to show off your curves. A bit of a train, because it is a ball gown, after all, and some finery, or detail around the bodice to call attention to your obvious assets. From where I stand, your curves appear to be natural, not cosmetically enhanced."

"I don't need too much attention," I said. "I don't know if Esmeralda told you, but we're actually here on a stealth mission."

"Are you smuggling drugs?"

"Do I look like a drug smuggler?"

"No. Which would make you an excellent one. Political secrets?"

"Stop grilling her," Esmeralda said, lounging on her purple plush chair as she texted.

"You won't be stealth if you don't fit in." Gareth walked to a rack, pulled a dress from it, and held it out to me. "Try on the rose gown. I think it will work. If so, I've got a bag that will match it perfectly. Can I ask you a private question?" He drew near to me, and I must admit I was intrigued.

"Yes."

He whispered, "Is Lady Joan married?"

"No."

"Boyfriend?"

"Not that I know of."

"Girlfriend?"

"I don't think so. Interested?"

"Yes."

"Do you have a significant other?"

"No. I'm just a cranky recluse."

"Can you curb your asshat ways and be a gentleman?"

"I doubt it."

"I've seen him do it before," Esmeralda said, sticking her nose into our conversation. "Gareth, you've got a crush on our Joan-y? What shall we do about this?"

"Food. What are you ladies doing tomorrow early afternoon?"

"The ladies have work to do," Mr. Philips said, joining our tight circle. "No time for holiday merriment."

"Bah humbug, Philips. They need to have a little fun before their grand night at the opera."

"Can I get in on this?" Joan poked her head into the circle.

"I'd like that," Gareth said.

"Good. What am I getting in on?"

"Cicchetti, wine, and a tour of the Rialto Market. A friend of mine's coming to town. She's an art historian, tracks down clues and mysteries and is very good with stealth missions. You should meet her, Lucky. I'll pick you up at La Princessa tomorrow at noon. Dress code: fashionably comfortable. Lovely working with you, Fredonians. I never listen to the gossip about you."

"What gossip?" I asked.

"Not you. From what I hear, you're not technically a Fredonian yet." He stood up and stretched. "My people will help you out. You're welcome."

"Thank you," Joan said.

"Send me the bill," Mr. Philips said.

"Of course. Lady Joan, a pleasure." He bowed, kissed her hand, then exited the cavernous room.

"When we first got here, I thought, oh great, here we are slumming it again." Joan peered down at her gown as an assistant unzipped the back of it, helping her out. "But then *this* happened. Between the suite at the Princessa, the ball gown dress-fitting thing, except for the ass-pinching thing, I think this trip is going exceptionally well. On an even more positive note, I can barely feel the bruise on my ass, and I think the Rescue Remedy is totally working."

"That's terrific, but we still haven't made contact with the priest impersonator," I said. "This isn't just fun and games. We're in Venezia on Mission Serenissima."

"Indeed. And ball gowns aren't cheap, ladies." Mr. Philips said. "Someone pass me the Scotch.

CHAPTER 10

Most people have three kinds of jeans: straight legged, boot cut, and flared at the ankle. I too have three kinds: fat, medium, and skinny. I've traveled up and down the scale, playing with fifteen pounds or so, and am usually pretty cool about that. As much as I liked to pride myself on being happy with my body image, if someone put my feet to the fire, I'd have to confess that when I was preparing to marry Nicholas for the *first* time, I dieted like a madwoman to stuff myself into a significantly smaller wedding dress. But ever since I walked down that aisle in Friedricksburg almost a month ago, I was hungry.

Which is why I couldn't be happier that following our tour of the famous, open-aired Rialto Market on a chilly, foggy December day, my ladies, Mr. Philips, Gareth, and I crowded around a wooden table in a busy trattoria sipping regional wines and noshing from small dishes filled with Venetian hors d'oeurves, aka cicchetti.

It seemed to me that Venetians lived life with brilliant abandonment – hanging out with their pals mid day, sampling delicious food items, and consuming them in bite-sizes until their taste buds sang hallelujah. Pinch me, I could get used to this.

"What did I just eat?" I sighed contentedly, dabbed the paper napkin to my mouth, and pointed to meaty crumbs left on a small, white ceramic dish embedded in a smear of thick, vibrant red sauce.

"Spicy fried meatballs." Gareth speared a hunk of bread topped in shaved parmesan, waving it in front of Joan's lips. "Try this, love."

"Delicious!" she said, between bites. "What is it?"

"Crab and mussel risotto. The flavors blend for an incomparable richness. Similar to the way you looked in the green gown I picked out for you. Did I tell you I'm attending the opera tonight?"

"I didn't know that."

"Perhaps we could—"

"Meet up for a drink thereafter?"

"I was thinking of something else." He winked at her.

"Oh." Joan leaned toward me, lifted her eyebrows, and whispered, "What's up with all the male attention? Perhaps I need to move to Italy."

"You're overdue in the male attention department. Kismet is catching up with you. Enjoy it," I said. "I like this way of eating. I could get used to it. Nick and I will move with you. We can eat these amazing mini meals every day, and never gain weight."

"That's the beauty of cicchetti: many tastes for many taste buds." Gareth looked up and waved at a woman who glanced around the small, packed room. "Zola! Over here!"

"Sorry I'm late!" The thirty-something woman waved cheerfully, making her way through the crowd toward us. She was beautiful: high cheekbones, impeccable light cocoa skin, her body curvy and fit. Her long, dark hair was fashioned in a hundred tiny braids, and twisted into a loose knot on the back of her head. She paused to greet an older, white-haired man sipping a cappuccino, savoring a dish of gelato. "Ciao mio amico," she said. "We must catch up."

"Who's that?" I asked.

"Someone you should get to know," Gareth said.

"Lady Zola Montbeliard! Bitch, what are you doing here?" Esmeralda jumped up, strode toward her, as they kissed on both cheeks and hugged.

"Esmeralda Castile von Haspburg, my sister from a different mister!" Zola pulled back and smiled. "Last I heard you were busy on a top secret project. What brings *you* to Venice?"

"Opera, mystery, and fashion," she said. "You?"

"Working on a historical art project in Verona that's also a bit of a puzzle."

"How so?" Esmeralda asked.

"Can't talk about that yet, or it wouldn't remain mysterious for much longer. By the way, Gareth, your eye for the design hidden in the painting's background was perceptive. I think you saved me a hundred research hours. Thank you!"

"Have you met Lucille?" Gareth asked.

"It is you!" Zola's eyes widened and she curtseyed. "You looked awfully familiar, Duchess, but I've had my head in the history books for too long. My apologies—where are my manners? So nice to meet you, Your Highness."

"Awesome to meet you as well." I waved my hand. "Call me Lucy. I'm not a 'Highness, or even a Duchess—'"

"She's not Dutch," Joan said. "Nice to see you Zola. It's been years."

"Lovely to see you as well, Joan. I heard all about you, Lucy, from my friend here, as well as what I've seen on social media."

"Let alone the unsocial media," Esmeralda said.

"The people of Fredonia dubbed you Lady with a

Fredonia Heart a few years back," Zola said and eyed me. "You're unassuming as well as pretty. No wonder Nicholas loves you to pieces."

A woman seated at the table next to us stopped flipping through her magazine, and squinted at me. "Signora with a Fredonia Heart?" She whispered under her breath, grabbing her phone and aiming it in my direction.

Mr. Philips frowned, his eyebrows slamming together. He pushed himself awkwardly to standing, stepped in front of her, and blocked her view. "My how the time slips away." He grabbed my arm and yanked me to my feet. "Lovely to see you, Lady Zola. Unfortunately, Lucille and I were just headed out to our next appointment."

"We were?"

"We are." He pulled his wallet from his overcoat. "How much do we owe?"

"Lunch is on me," Gareth said.

"Thank you. We'll see you tonight, I trust?"

"Wouldn't miss it." He stared pie-eyed at Joan.

"Ciao ciao," Mr. Philips said. "See you back at the hotel, ladies. Don't dally."

Mr. Philips hustled me through the packed lunch crowd, down the hallway toward the bathrooms.

"I think at this point you should know that if I need to use the facilities, I'll ask."

"Thoughtful of you," he said as we squeezed past bins of vegetables and stacks of wine boxes. "I'm more concerned about the possibility of being swarmed by the press. If that persistent woman managed to snap a pic, this exit will be less packed with reporters than the front."

"It's been a minute. How quickly could they get here?"

"They're already here, Lucille. That woman *is* the tabloid press. These days, it seems like everyone is. Let's get out of here while we can," he said as we squeezed out the back door.

CHAPTER 11

We made our way down a small side street, Mr. Philips hurrying me as fast as a pissed off grade school teacher walking a naughty ten-year-old boy to the principle's office.

"Why so frantic, Philips? Besides that opportunistic woman with crappy boundaries, I thought we were enjoying our outing."

"Did you see the tabloid flipped open on her table? The one she was reading?"

"No. I was trying to figure out what spices they put in the fried meatballs and the sauce. I think Nick would love the recipe."

"You need to worry about the sauce that's smeared across page two of *All Right Magazine*. The headline read,

'**ON WHOSE DIME?**
LUCY ABANDONS FREDONIA AS PRINCE NICHOLAS SERVES GUARD DUTY.'

It was accompanied by a photo of you, the ladies, and myself boarding Royal Nana's jet yesterday morning."

"How would they know that? Who would tip them off?"

"The guy servicing the royal jet, the caterer who delivered the snacks for our trip. Anyone. Everyone. What does it matter? As soon as someone forwards a photo of you in Venice to that rag, the paparazzi will descend upon us, and hound our every step. That will slow down our mission to get you unwed and greatly displease Her Royal Highness. She's not going to live forever you know."

"Is she okay?"

"Yes, and we want to keep it that way." He stopped walking, pausing to catch his breath, and eyed me. "Does your coat have a hood?"

"Do I look like I'm snowmobiling?"

"No." He pulled his warm woolen scarf from around his neck and handed it to me. "Wrap this over your head."

"Do I have to?"

"Yes."

"Fine." I pulled it on, knotting it under my chin, and crinkling my nose. "Your man scarf reeks of cologne. It's stronger than the smell of a fifteen-year-old boy who just bought his first bottle of Axe. I realize that it's probably expensive—the undercurrents are warm with spicy citrus and musk. Do you bathe in this stuff? Might I suggest you slap it on a bit more sparingly? My hair will smell exactly like you. I'll have to wash it before the opera tonight."

"It's Dior. You could do worse. We're headed back to the hotel. I need to regroup, rest my back, and get you out of sight before someone recognizes you."

"Crap, we're too late!" I stopped in my tracks, jabbing my finger in the direction of a dock approximately fifty yards away from us. "Over there. See the sixty-something couple in matching faux fur trimmed jackets stepping out of that swank gondola? That's the Duke and Duchess of Holstein LaGorpe."

"Weren't they at your wedding?"

"Which one?"

"Any. I can't keep up."

"Yes," I said. "My first wedding to Nicholas in Friedricksburg. I'd recognize the smug looks on their overly-Botoxed faces anywhere. I thought I'd need a bottle of Windex to wipe off the thick smear of condescension when Nicholas was kidnapped, leaving me high and dry at the church. You'd have thought I'd stepped in a pile of dog poo before I entered the cathedral and ground it into the white runner with every delicate step on my way toward the altar."

"They're headed in our direction. Don't look at them."

"I already looked at them! We're going to cross paths in T minus thirty seconds. Crap! They're totally going to recognize me." I stopped in my tracks, glancing around for an escape route, or a hiding place, or a sinkhole to open in the ground beneath me, and magically swallow me whole.

"They will if you stand there like a speed bump." He pushed his hand into the small of my back, propelling me forward. "Move."

I stumbled but caught myself. "What if they recognize *you*? They'll stop to say hello, and quickly figure out that the woman under the aromatic head scarf is me—Lucille Trabbicio, part-time wife to Prince Nicholas of Fredonia."

"That might not happen if you keep walking."

"It will. These kinds of people have a nose for gossip, and right now, I'm a veritable bouquet. They'll say hi to you and then ID me. We'll have one of those enormously uncomfortable moments where we make forced small talk as they eye each other knowingly. The second we fake promise to hang out with them back in Fredonia, they'll text all their friends, and plant the seed that you and I are conducting a sordid, clandestine May-December affair."

"I'm flattered, Lucille," Mr. Philips said. "I haven't been involved in anything sordid in quite a while. Pick up your feet and move it along."

"The gossips will yammer on about our very predictable older man younger woman romance. It will be a scandal. Like Princess Margaret and Peter Townsend in Great Britain back in the 1950s."

"Their age difference was fifteen years." Mr. Philips said. "Ours is more like forty five. I don't think anyone will buy it."

"What does it matter?" I kept my head down and stared at my feet. "The palace won't take kindly to this kerfuffle. God knows what they'll do to me. I've seen that dungeon, and it is a dark and dismal place. They'll probably send you off as envoy to Belgium, or something, and even though you're practically a father figure to me, I won't see you for two years. Then people will ask me how you are, and I'll say, honestly, that I don't have a clue. Because while of course I'll miss you, let's face it, no matter how badly I stank of your expensive, fancy men's cologne, we were never an item. But no one will believe me, and I'll be hit with those knowing looks and the wink-winks from older men wherever I go. Octogenarian men with liver spots who think that they can fill your sturdy, expensive wing-tipped shoes. My life will become hell." I wrung my hands. "And I will be cursed with the stinky hint of royal scandal forever!"

"I rather like Belgium."

"Of course you do. Is it the waffles or the Brussels sprouts?"

"What are you talking about?"

"Never mind."

"Your worries are over. The Duke and Duchess of

79

Holstein LaGorpe have turned a corner," he said. "They're gone."

"Thank God!" I plucked at the scarf on my head, desperate to yank it off.

"Keep it on until we get inside the hotel," he said.

"Easy for you to say. It's okay if you smell like an expensive older man who bathes in Dior. No one will blink an eye." My gaze was drawn toward a guy in a small dinghy in the canal who puttered slowly in our direction, almost as if he was following us. "Don't look now, Philips, but over my shoulder at nine o'clock. There's a man in a long raincoat in a small, unassuming boat. I've seen him before. I think he's tailing us."

"The *last* thing I'll be doing is checking him out. No doubt he's yet another member of the press, or a Fredonia-phile who has spotted you. We need to save our energy to track down the imposter priest tonight at the opera."

Lucky for me, the guy in the boat turned down a side canal, and disappeared from sight. "Let's say we find the poser priest. Besides appealing to his sense of right and wrong, his higher self, how will we get him to sign Royal Nana's affidavit? Wait a minute. I've got an idea... My ladies in waiting are pretty good with dicey situations. Joan can corner him in the theater's lobby and ask for directions to the lavatory. I'll sneak up behind him, shove my finger in the back of his kidney area, and tell him to walk to a deserted corridor ahead of us."

"He's going to be intimidated by your slender finger?"

"It will feel like the barrel of a gun. I can poke pretty hard, you know."

"A very skinny gun."

"Fine, I'll use two fingers. If he puts up a fuss, Esmeralda can deck him."

"She doesn't like physical combat."

"Then she can flash her boobs. That'll cause a ruckus, and throw some attention in our direction. I'll start screaming, 'Priest Imposter! Marriage Stealer! Whatever you do, don't get married by this man because you'll regret it!' I think that will force Milton Mertz to take us seriously."

"I've got a more impressive idea," he said.

"What's more impressive than Esmeralda flashing her boobs?"

"A paycheck. I've been authorized to hand Milton Mertz a tidy sum of Euros for his John Hancock on that document. As much as I adore you, Lucille, this is still, after all, palace business. If you're not unmarried by the time you return to Fredonia, you'll lose your part-time job as spokes model for Friedricksburgh, you won't be allowed to legally marry Prince Nicholas, and Royal Nana will have my head."

CHAPTER 12

I glanced up at the luxurious banner hanging down from the royal balcony positioned high above the theatre's entrance, the name of the holiday opera, *Amahl and the Night Visitors* stamped in vibrant colors into its fabric, and felt somewhat awestruck.

I'd been to my share of concerts. I partied at Buddy Guy's Legends, the classic house of blues, in Chicago. I'd schlepped up to Alpine Valley in Elkhorn, Wisconsin with my BFF, Alida a few years back to take in a Pearl Jam concert, but this was the first time I had ever attended an opera.

Duchess Edith's box was situated in the balcony's first row. The air felt different up here. Magical. Rarified. Like the gorgeous chandelier on the ceiling high above us was sprinkling pixie dust into the air above our heads.

Our posse of usual suspects was joined tonight by two newcomers: Gareth Trent, British ex-pat fashion designer gazed at Joan like he was a cat and she was a delectable morsel that he wished to chase, play with, and conquer. Lady Zola Montbeliard had forgiven our bad manners this afternoon at the trattoria, and when we extended her an invitation, chosen to join us in Duchess Edith's opera box.

"I still can't believe I'm at the opera in Venice, Italy," I said. "It's so luxurious."

"It's a quaint theatre," Joan said. "Intimate in scope, but that will make it easier for us to spot Milton Mertz."

"That is if he shows tonight," Esmeralda said.

"He's got to show," I said. "It's his brother's big night, after all."

"Not everybody values their family members the way you do, Lucille," Mr. Philips said.

"Don't rain on my parade. I won't allow you to ruin this for me."

A woman in the box adjacent to us swiveled her large coiffed head in our direction, and frowned. "Please be quiet and don't ruin it for the rest of us."

"Sorry!" Joan and I whispered.

We settled into our seats and enjoyed the first half hour of *Amahl and the Night Visitors*. This was a relatively new holiday classic that clocked in at a little under an hour, a perfect length for the children or someone like me who had a short attention span.

"Andrea Mertzolio's really killing it tonight as King Kaspar," Joan said. "He's a talented tenor."

"I think I've heard of Andrea before," Zola said. "Didn't he portray Spoletta, the police agent, in Tosca last spring?"

"I'll Google it when we're in a cell friendly zone," Esmeralda said. "But I doubt he ever played a role higher than third spear carrier from the left."

I looked around at our crew and couldn't help but smile: we cleaned up nice. Joan wore Gareth's emerald green ball gown that highlighted her porcelain skin. Mr. Philip Philips shone in his go-to black tuxedo with his spit polished shoes, his crinkly crystal blue eyes sparkling. Zola's dress was long, fitted, a smoking tangerine that brought out the hazel in her eyes. Esmeralda donned a low cut number in her signature red, her cleavage front and center, worthy of notice, and probably its own zip code.

I wore the rose colored silk frock that Gareth had picked for me. Soft petals of delicate see-through fabric accentuated the sturdier damask silk of the bust, the waistline nipped in, the curves of the gown hugging my hips, sliding down my thighs like a caress from a contented lover. Which totally made me think of Nick.

I'd texted him earlier when we were back at the Princessa hotel getting dolled up for our exciting night out. "In Venice," I typed. "Thinking of Carnival. Missing you horribly. Your Lucy." A "Delivered" note popped up on my screen, but Nick never texted back.

"I'm impressed," Joan said, tapping me on the shoulder. It brought me back to reality for a moment. "These are the best seats I've ever sat in at an opera. We're close enough to view the expressions on the actors' faces. The music is divine, and the sound system perfecto. Kudos to Duchess Edith on knowing which art house to patronize."

"She's a force to be reckoned with," Mr. Philips said. "There's a reason she's called the Teflon Dame."

"I heard that rumor on more than one occasion," Esmeralda said.

The woman in the adjacent opera box swiveled her head in our direction, pressed a stern finger to her pursed lips, and schussed us.

"Sorry!" Joan and I whispered.

It was that point in the musical story unfolding on the stage where Amahl's widowed mother contemplated taking advantage of the visiting Kings. She reasoned that they had so much and she had so little, and besides, how could they ever prove she'd stolen from them? I knew what it was like to be down on your luck, but I'd always worked incredibly hard to make an honest living. Silly as it sounds I rooted for the mother to say 'No' to her desires, when it dawned on me—I was fighting my own.

I knew that this was a cell phone free zone, but my fingers were itchy, and my emotions were bouncing between morose and exhilarated. I wanted, no—*I needed*— to talk to Nick. He was my go-to guy, my best friend. I wished I could hear his voice. Get his input. What did he think: would we apprehend the priest impersonator tonight and bring him to justice? Would this whole drama calm down and my stomach stop doing flip-flops? Or perhaps those were just the spicy meatballs messing with me.

If I couldn't hear him, a text or an email would do. All the sensible and polite voices in my head said, 'No, no, Lucy Marie. Take a chill pill. Don't do this.' But I simply couldn't resist for one second longer. I dug through my matching silk bag, and pulled out my phone.

Mr. Philips glared at me and shook his head.

"Emotional emergency," I said, giving into the rush of feelings as I texted Nick. "Are you all right? Are they feeding you?" But I received no reassuring reply. I held onto the warm device and silently willed him to text me back. But it didn't vibrate or hum and I couldn't help but feel even more down in the dumps.

In the opera unfolding on the stage, Amahl's mother was stealing from the Kings. I felt so bad that she'd hit this all time personal low, but secretly hoped she'd get her shit together, realize she'd done a terrible thing, make everything right, and find redemption. And then I wondered what Nick was doing.

My brain chattered away, telling me that he was busy on guard duty performing tedious, boring tasks, and quite possibly courageous ones. I shut my eyes and imagined him on the Air Ambulance helicopter rescuing distressed boaters who had capsized in the Mediterranean, or a pair of hikers who had taken a wrong turn on a mountainous trail in the Alps and gotten hopelessly lost. Either option meant that he'd most likely be subjected to bitterly cold weather, and I hoped his regulation uniform included a long-sleeved moisture-resistant thermal T-shirt to keep him warm.

That's when a memory of just how hot he looked when he was wearing nothing but a long-sleeved T-shirt and his undies struck my brain like a asteroid hitting a trailer park in the desert. I'd returned from yet another stupid wedding dress fitting in Friedricksburg, collapsed onto my bed and curled up with my dog, Tulip.

She licked my face as we cuddled. "A royal wedding carries impossibly high expectations and it's simply too much, Tulip," I said, scratching her blond head. "The bridesmaids' dresses have to be perfect. My gown has to be as lovely as other royal brides', but not too spectacular as people will say I'm trying to outshine them. Normally, I wouldn't give a rat's ass about any of this, but I'm marrying into a royal family, and apparently a rat's ass must be sacrificed to get this deed done."

She looked at me, passed a little wind, sighed, and closed her eyes.

I fanned my face. "I'm with you, sister."

Nick stepped into the room in-between meetings and regarded me and the dog on the bed with a quizzical look on his face. "Hello?"

Tulip jumped off the bed and ran to greet him.

"I didn't do that," I said. "It wasn't me."

"Of course." Nick scratched her ears.

"It was the dog."

"I know." He walked over and kissed me on the forehead.

"But you're the one who has mascara stains around your eyes. Not the dog."

"Point taken. Just go. You've got work to do. The last thing you need is to cheer up your ridiculously emotional bride-to-be."

"On the contrary darling." He took my hand, weaved his fingers between mine, then pulled them to his lips and kissed them. "I'll have nothing in my life of any substance if I don't have you. If my girl needs cheering up, I am up for the task."

"For real?"

"For real. What needs to happen to put a smile on your face? Chocolates? Flowers? Dinner at the romantic French restaurant in old town: La Creperie? Name it—it's yours."

I wiped my tears away and eyed his high cheekbones, the cleft in his chin you could hide a nickel in, the blackest of hair with that errant lock that hung over his forehead that made a girl's hands itch to smooth it back onto his head and kiss him. And then there were his shoulders: Firm. Muscular. Delectable. And let's not get started on his six-pack abs or his ridiculously gorgeous ass. "Strip for me, Nicholas."

He cocked a black eyebrow at me. "You'd prefer me stripping to a five course gourmet meal at a five star French restaurant?"

"Yes."

"Your wish is my command, my princess."

And strip he did.

First his coat. Then he played with unbuttoning his pinstriped shirt. Slowly. Very slowly The dress pants were next. He teased me with the zipper. Up and down until I begged him to take it off, just take it all off. At last he stood in front of me wearing only his long-sleeve tight cotton T-shirt that hugged his biceps, triceps, ripped shoulders and chest muscles.

I could practically hear the angels sing, heard sweet Jesus

welcome me home, and dabbed away a bit of drool that had arrived unceremoniously at the corners of my mouth. "You're so hot," I said, leaning back on the pillows on our feathertop bed as I gazed into his eyes and parted my knees for him.

"You're hotter." He climbed on top of me, straddling me, pulling my blouse over my head, and unzipping my jeans.

"No, you are." I fumbled with his long-sleeved T-shirt at the same time he yanked my pants down my legs, our breath quickening. Step aside David Beckham. Take a back seat David Gandy. My Nick could be a cover model for high-end male underwear.

And now, here in this gorgeous opera house, it felt like forever since I'd squeezed his buff arms, gazed into his gorgeous blue eyes, and ran my hand over his tight ass. Good God, I felt like I was going cold turkey. This was just as bad as quitting caffeine or chocolate. I fanned my face. "Is it hot in here?"

"No," Esmeralda said.

I closed my eyes and remembered Nick's lips on mine, the scruff of his five o'clock shadow scraping my skin as he kissed my face and worked his way down: my collar bones, my breasts, the softness of my stomach, my hips, and dove lower. Did he miss me as much as I missed him?

"Oh my God!" Joan leaned forward with opera glasses held tightly to her face. "I spotted the guy who married you."

My eyes popped open. "Holy crap! Nicholas is here?"

"No. But Milton Mertz is. He's seated two thirds of the way away from the stage. On the far right, and if I squint I bet I can make out the row... number thirty-five."

"Hand me the glasses," Mr. Philips said. She passed them over, and he peered through them. "Good call! That is Milton Mertz, priest impersonator in the flesh."

"What do we do now?" I asked.

He glanced at the vintage gold Rolex on his wrist. "The

opera's ending in around ten minutes. I have the paperwork in my pocket. Lucy, you and I will discretely leave the box now and position ourselves in a quiet part of the foyer to 'greet' Milton Mertz. I'll flash him the check I'm prepared to hand him in exchange for his signature. I think he'll say 'Yes.' Then we can relocate backstage to a private dressing room to conduct the transaction."

"But what if he sees us and tries to escape?"

"Zola and I will run interference," Esmeralda said. "We'll leave the box a few minutes after you, so as not to call attention to our departure, and position ourselves in the middle of the room as your back up."

"There will be mobs of people milling about, pulling on their coats, preparing to leave," I said. "Remember. Milton Mertz looks like the nicest man in the world. Kind eyes. Unassuming physique. But I suspect he's a wolf in sheep's clothing. Don't forget, I bought his kind words and his generosity of spirit. But he's not an easy study. Something else is going on with that guy. He must have deep dark secrets that make him tick. What if he sneaks around you and slips out an exit door?"

"Joan and I will be stationed at the exit doors," Gareth said. "Two of my assistants are in the audience tonight. I'm texting them right now and they'll cover additional exits."

"Mission Serenissima commences," Mr. Philips said. "Let's go, Lucille."

My phone chirped. "Wait a second. That could be Nick."

"Not now," Mr. Philips said.

"But it could be important." My finger was poised to hit the phone's button.

"I doubt it." Esmeralda snatched the phone from my hands so fast she could have been a professional pickpocket.

"No. That's mine. Give it back to me."

She shook her head and eyed the screen. "It's from Nicholas."

"I figured as much. Hand it to me!"

"No. You need to go. Now!"

"What if something is wrong with him? What if he's been hurt, and he needs me to fly to his side and rescue him? Read me his text."

"He says he too is in Italy, close by—he can't say where—"

"What if Nicholas is lying cold and alone in a deserted battle field with a terrible wound, and we need to rescue him before it's too late?" I wrung my hands.

"It says here that he and the rest of the Air Ambulance crew are at base, enjoying hearty stews, bread and cheese."

"That doesn't mean he's not in harm's way."

She eyed my phone. "They're playing a double feature tonight: the movie *Heat* with Sandra Bullock and Melissa McCarthy and *Wedding Crashers* with Vince Vaughn and Owen Wilson."

"Give me my phone."

"No." She shoved it down her cleavage where it disappeared.

"It will get lost down there and never come back."

Esmerelda clamped onto my arms and shook me. "Snap out of it, Lucy. You're love struck, and thinking with your emotions instead of your practical brain. Catch the priest imposter. Get the paperwork signed. I'll give you your phone back when the mission's accomplished."

"You drive a mean bargain." I tossed my hair dramatically over my shoulder, stood up, and followed Mr. Philips out of the cushy opera box.

CHAPTER 13

Mr. Philips' plan to intercept the priest impersonator was going exactly as planned. We had positioned ourselves in the lobby approximately twelve feet from the exit door as the thunderous applause and cries of "Bravo! Bravo!" from the exuberant audience thundered around us.

Esmeralda and Joan stood behind us fanned out on diagonals. Zola, Gareth, and his people manned four of the theatre's exit doors. People piled out, happy, chatting in Italian, bandying about words like "Bellissima," and "Meraviglioso." Another five minutes ticked by and I realized there was just one small problem.

"I don't see him," I said, peering over the bustle of the excited audience, the women in their gorgeous gowns, the men wearing their finest cut suits, and the well-dressed children clamoring for attention, food, and sleep.

"He has to come out, eventually," Mr. Philips said, as we were jostled by the crush of the crowd. "Why don't you check in with the ladies?"

I stood on my tiptoes, waving my hand high in the air in Joan's direction. "Seen Mertz?"

She shook her head. 'No.'

I asked Esmeralda the same question and earned the same result.

I kept my eagle eye on the door between the auditorium and the foyer as another five minutes ground by. Two women regarded me suspiciously, a pimply teenage boy flirted with me, and three dapper men with liver spots winked and slipped me their cards, making me wonder if that nasty Duke and Duchess Holstein-Gorpe had indeed spotted us and were already spreading false rumors. I tapped the toe of my low-heeled pump on the ground and glared at Mr. Philips. "Where is he?"

"I don't know. From his position in the theatre, I'd have predicted he'd be out by now."

I glanced in Zola's direction and waved at her, catching her attention. "Seen Mertz?"

"No," she shrugged.

I scratched my head, and suddenly my brain lit up like I'd downed a doppio espresso and a triple chocolate brownie. I swiveled, pushing my way through the well-heeled crowd, past Mr. Philips, and headed back toward the auditorium.

"Where are you going?" he asked.

"I'm going to find the priest impersonator."

"He's got to come out these doors. Even if he's disguised as a nun in *The Sound of Music*, we'll spot him. The place is emptying out."

"No we won't." I paused at a banquette situated adjacent to the doors leading from the foyer back into the theatre. I looked up at the large vase propped on it filled with a rich holiday bouquet of orchids, roses, and twigs with red berries. I stood on my tiptoes, grabbed a few flowers, and shook the water from their stems onto the floor. "Milton Mertz would have wanted to congratulate his brother in person. He went backstage. I'm going to find him."

I slipped back inside the auditorium and made my way down a side aisle. I paused, snatched some festive ribbons off a Christmas tree next to a wall, and wrapped them around the stems of the flowers I'd confiscated. Now they could pass for a proper bouquet.

I snuck a peek at our playbill before approaching the side entrance leading to the back of the stage. I told the guard I was a distant cousin to Sophia Romano, the actress who played the mother, and was so very excited to tell her "Brava" in person. I pushed the point home by batting my eyes and slipping him a twenty Euro note.

Entering the backstage of an opera house might have been cake, but trying to figure out the lay of the land was a completely different story. There was a quiet but palpable post-performance energy behind the scenes: art department members carried props, wardrobe techs pushed racks of clothes to their designated holding area between shows. Tonight's performance might have been over but the post-production clean up paved the way for the next show to run smoothly. Everyone seemed to have a purpose; knew exactly what to do and where to go.

Funny, I felt the same way about my life. If I could find Mertz, and get my affidavit signed, I too could have a designated path. I could finally marry my beloved Nicholas, for good, for real, forever. Besides, it was Christmas and people wanted miracles. George Bailey got his in *It's a Wonderful Life* and I needed my Happily Ever After as well.

I made my way past a smattering of fans chatting with actors, their faces thick with theatrical makeup. I walked past dressing rooms with signs indicating the surnames of the performers sharing the tiny chambers.

I was deep into the bowels of the theatre when I spotted a door cracked open, a sign on it that read, "RE" with a crown emblazoned on top. Laughter emanated into the already boisterous backstage corridor. I leaned back against the adjacent wall so as not to call attention to myself, trying to peek inside.

"Re translates to King," Mr. Philips whispered in my ear.

I jumped six inches as my hand flew to my chest. "Thank you for the heart attack. How did you get backstage?"

"The guard was occupied with you, so I snuck in the other entrance. Is Milton in there with his brother the tenor?"

"I don't know. I don't have a clear view."

A familiar voice spoke from behind the door. "I am so proud of you, Andrea. Unfortunately, I've got to get going. We'll meet up after the New Year's, yes?"

"Just tell me where and when. Thanks for coming. I know you've got a lot going on. I can't tell you how much it means to have you here."

I peeked through the crack and got an eyeful: Milton Mertz, poser, priest imposter—formerly known as Father McGillicuddy—hugged his brother affectionately. I couldn't help but be a little jealous and confused all at the same time. Milton looked so kind. Why did he get to have a family? Why did they look like they were having so much fun? Why was I stuck here in this corridor with an older man breathing over my shoulder whom I adored, but nonetheless reeked of Dior?

"Follow me!" Mr. Philips latched onto my arm, tugging me a few feet away from the dressing room. We crouched behind a large wheeled rack of clothes.

"I don't understand why we're hiding. It's him and he's leaving. We need to confront him now, or he'll be lost to us again."

"I don't want your picture being snapped if there's a confrontation. Stay here. I'll handle this." Mr. Philips straightened back up. Suddenly he cringed and cried out in pain.

"What's wrong?"

"My back went out!"

"Crap! Are you okay?"

"Don't know," he said, wincing.

"Signore!" A guard approached us, frowning. "No-no! Signore, non ti è permessdi essere qui!"

"Hand me the affidavit," I whispered, digging through my purse.

Mr. Philips slipped the neatly folded document from his pocket, and passed it to me.

I tucked it in my pretty bag and passed him a sample-sized bottle of ibuprofen. "They're over the counter. Take two with water. Feel better."

"Good luck," he said, slamming back the pills.

"Thank you. With any luck I'll get his signature and we can put Mission Serenissima to bed. Don't get arrested. Be nice to the guard. If push comes to shove, bat your eyes and slip him a few Euros." I slipped down the hallway after Milton Mertz, leaving Philips to deal with the crabby guy in the uniform.

CHAPTER 14

I was surprised how many byzantine passageways and staircases the Venice Opera House had. It felt like I followed Milton Mertz down all of them, trying my very best to stay one short turn behind him.

I paused when he paused, flattening my back against unadorned walls lit only by a singular dim bulb overhead. I listened for his signature raspy breath because with this course of action I had no visual clues.

Maybe I should have just hollered his name. Perhaps I should have simply said, 'Hey, remember me? I'm Lucy Marie Trabbicio, the chick you showed kindness to when I stopped by the St. Francis of Assisi Sanctuary. I was the bride in the pretty dress who you married to Prince Nicholas. Did you know that you weren't palace approved to conduct royal Fredonia weddings? Did you know you would ruin the beginning of my married life? Because if you did, that was a rotten thing to do.'

I picked up the pace, poked my head around a corner, and stared at him as he shuffled away from me. I longed to holler my truth, but I kept my mouth shut, my eyes on the prize:

the signed affidavit to renounce my previous 'technical' marriage and free me to marry Nick again.

So when Milton Mertz, aka, Father McGillicuddy, popped out a back exit of the opera house and walked into an alleyway around 10:30 pm on this foggy, damp, cold-in -my-bones night, I too left the building and followed him, shivering.

I lingered behind, keeping my distance as he made his way through the twists and turns of the narrow lanes of the city, skirting along the edges of the canals. When I turned a corner, I spotted him talking with a man wearing a raincoat who stood in a small boat tied to a weathered dock.

Goosebumps erupted on my arms as I realized it was the same guy I'd seen peering up at me with binoculars at the Hotel Princessa. The man who had followed me when I left the Trattoria. Even worse, this stalker was now holding his hand out to the priest impersonator and helping him board the boat. Soon the poser would be gone again, and I couldn't hold my tongue any longer. "Father McGillicuddy!" I hollered.

He looked at me oddly, and then shook his head in disbelief. "Lucy?"

"Yes. Is your name McGillicuddy or should I call you Milton Mertz?" I asked, strolling toward him.

"Either is fine. I go by both. What are you doing in Venezia?"

"We need to get going, Milton," the man in the boat said, unhooking the ropes that secured the vessel to the dock. "I fear you've opened up a can of worms."

"Not so fast." I pulled the affidavit from my purse. "The marriage you performed for Prince Nicholas and me didn't stick. The Royal Church of Fredonia won't sanction it. You're not allowed to perform royal marriages."

"Of course I can perform marriages," he said.

"*Royal* marriages. Archbishop Causesdesperdues said that you are not a sanctioned priest."

"Archbishop Causesdesperdues can be a bit of an asshat."

"Tell me about it. Who sends a telegram to someone on their honeymoon informing them that they are not really wed?"

"He did that?"

I nodded. "It was horrible."

"I bet. He's always been an alarmist as well as a wet blanket."

"I couldn't agree more. Nonetheless, the palace says my union to Nicholas won't hold up in the royal church, but unfortunately, it could be upheld in a court of law. Therefore I am stuck. A bride without a groom. A marriage that must be undone."

"This is one of the reasons why I had to leave the church," he said. "All the legal-ese and antiquated laws. It wasn't a decision I was happy about."

The man in the boat started the engine. "I hate to cut this short, but they're expecting us, and we're not authorized to bring anyone with us."

"I beg you, Father McGillicuddy," I said. "If you ever felt bad for a girl in need, a woman down on her luck, please do me one more kindness; one last favor."

"Yes, yes, my child." He made the sign of the cross. "Go ahead and confess your sins."

"That's not the favor." I pulled the affidavit from my purse, and extended it toward him over the murky canal waters. "I hold in my hand an affidavit crafted by Her Royal Highness Marie Susannah Clothilde Timmel's advisers. I've been assured that if you sign this document, I will be legally unmarried, which will then allow me to royally wed Nicholas again, for real this time. Would you do that for me? Would you, in the spirit of Christmas and all the good things in this world put your John Hancock on this document that affirms I am not religiously, or legally wed to Prince Nicholas Frederick Timmel of Fredonia? That I have never been wed to Prince Nicholas Frederick Timmel of Fredonia?"

"Of course. Hand it to me."

I passed it to him, breathing a sigh of relief, tears welling in my eyes. At last this nightmare would be over. I started wondering what kind of wedding dress I could wear to my next marriage ceremony and I didn't even break out in hives at the thought. I had done the big poofy dress—no wait— that was when I almost married Cristoph. I had followed that up with a lovely silk batiste gown. I was currently blanking on the details of last dress I wore to the chapel in Friedricks- burg, but considering all the stress I'd been under lately, I didn't think anyone would hold that against me.

But Milton Mertz stood frozen, staring at the document as the boat swayed.

"What's wrong?" I asked. "Do you need a pen?"

"I'm skimming it, Lucy. Always check the fine print on these legal documents. Have to make sure HRH isn't selling me her portion of an unwanted timeshare. I got involved with one of those schemes once and it wasn't pleasant."

"We need to get out of here, Milton," the man said, and revved the motor.

"Yes, yes," he said, signing the document with a flourish, and extending it toward me.

I leaned down, my hand shaking, and took it from him.

"I'm sorry for any pain I might have cause you, Lucy," Milton said as the boat puttered away. "That was never my intent."

"Good to know," I said, waving at him. "What will you do now? Where will you go?"

"Don't tell her that Milton," the boat's captain said. "That's on a need to know basis."

"If you're ever in Cortina d'Ampresszo, look me up," Milton said. "I'll be on sabbatical there for a while."

"It's not a sabbatical. And I told you not to tell her that."

"Thank you Father McGillicuddy," I said. "Merry Christmas!"

He waved at me as they rounded a bend and disappeared from sight, the sounds of the puttering motor trailing off.

I looked at the signed affidavit in my cold, clammy, shaking hand, and realized my marital nightmare was over. I could marry my beloved Nicholas. I could have royally wed sex with him, and maybe some day we'd adopt another puppy or two, or perhaps a cat, and who knows, even have a kid. I burst into tears.

"Lucy! Is that you, bitch?!" Esmeralda popped her head around the corner of an old building accompanied by Joan, Zola, and Mr. Philips who limped behind them.

"Yes! Did you bring my coat? I'm freezing!" I shivered, wrapped my arms around my shoulders and gave myself a hug.

"Did you get the document signed?" Mr. Philips asked.

"I did."

"Are you in one piece?"

"I am. How's your back?"

"I'll live."

"Yay!" Joan said. "We must go celebrate! Even better, I have Prince Harry's Scotch in my purse." She pulled the silver flask from her bag, knocked back a shot, and handed it to Zola.

Esmeralda's cleavage buzzed. She pulled out my phone and stared at the screen. "That's Nick, again. He's been texting you non-stop."

"Hand me the phone, please."

"Not until I see the document," Esmeralda said. "That was our deal after all."

Zola downed a shot of Prince Harry's and fanned her lips. "That's prime shelf," she said, passing it to Esmeralda.

"Hand it to me! I need to see his texts. They might be important. You said you'd give it back as soon as I got the paperwork signed."

"Anything for you, my friend, the future Duchess of Friedricksburg." Esmeralda juggled the flask and tossed me the phone. "Just promise me I don't have to be a bridesmaid again."

My phone spiraled through the air toward me as I reached my free hand to catch it. "Why don't you want to be a bridesmaid…" But no matter how high I stretched my arm, or stood on my tippy toes, the device sailed above my reach, toward the waters of the dark Venice canal. And I did the only thing that a distraught girl who missed her fiancé could do when faced with a crisis of watery proportions: I leapt high in the air in a Herculean attempt to grab it.

And grab it I did: one hand held the phone, my other clutched the affidavit. Time slowed down as I glanced down and saw both my feet were off the dock and I realized I wouldn't be landing on solid ground. I gazed at the murky dark waters of the Venice canal that rapidly approached my face, shut my eyes, and braced for a full water immersion.

The splash was impressive.

CHAPTER 15

"How lucky were we that Mertz disclosed his next destination was Cortina d'Ampresszo," Esmeralda said. "Royal Nana's advisors are researching nearby compounds where he might be residing with his secret group."

Mr. Philips hired a driver who drove us the next morning in an SUV equipped with monster snow tires from Venice to this popular ski resort town high in the Italian Alps.

Now I stood in the crowded chairlift line staring up at the daunting mountain in front of us. "How long does one's arm ache after a tetanus shot?" I shivered, in spite of the soft, eggshell white lambswool scarf wrapped three times around my neck, and my blush-colored Gareth Trent designer ski jacket that hugged my upper body.

"They gave you more than a tetanus booster," Joan said. "Do you even know what's in the waters of the Venice canals? It's filled with fec—"

I stuck my fingers in my ears. "La, la, la, don't want to know the details. All I know is that the water's got something in it that dissolves fresh ink on paper. The affidavit is ruined, useless, a soggy, disintegrated piece of paper."

"Which is why we're here," Esmeralda said.

"I checked out local Air BnB's and narrowed it down to two places," Zola said. "I've forwarded Google maps of both to each of your cell phones and printed paper copies for backup."

"Because we know what happens to old-fashioned paper copies," Esmeralda said.

"If you hadn't confiscated my tech savvy smartphone and stuffed it in your sweaty cleavage, I might be marrying Nicholas right now instead of trying to get Milton Mertz's signature yet again!" I flipped her my middle finger.

A few women who resembled pastel-colored marshmallows on sticks turned in our direction and gave me the once over.

"Knock it off," Esmeralda said. "Unlike the other chicks waiting in the lift line behind us, we aren't here simply to have fun and flirt with the cute skier boys.

"Fine." The line for the ski lift shuffled forward, and I shivered again. "Crap, it's cold up here."

"It's the winds," Joan said, standing behind me next to Zola. "It might read minus five degrees Celsius but the wind chill makes it feel more like minus ten. It's not going to get any warmer on top of the mountain. Should we go back to the lodge and grab more layers?"

"No," Esmeralda said, stamping her skis of excess snow as she stood on my right. "We have to bite the bullet, toughen up, stick it to the man, and complete this mission. As much as I enjoy hanging out with you ladies, I have pressing business waiting for me back in Fredonia. We need to get Lucy unmarried and then remarried quickly."

"We all have work to get back to," Joan said. "Why do we have to 'stick it to the man?'"

"Because it sounds bad ass," Zola said. "Bad ass-ery is Esmeralda's signature super power when she's stressed out."

"I am not stressed out," Esmeralda said.

"You are totally stressed out," Zola said. "Case in point you had stress sex with our chauffeur after we checked into the chalet."

"How do you know?"

"I saw you making out in the hallway and then he followed you into your suite. The loud banging sounds in my adjoining room were the third clue."

"That was hot Italian chauffeur sex. Not stress sex."

"It's both. You also had two hot toddies at the bar before we rented skis," Zola said.

"Do you fancy yourself to be Agatha Christie?" Esmeralda asked.

"No. I lean toward Nancy Drew."

"Hot chauffeur. Hot toddies. Clearly the theme is 'hot' because I am chilly," Esmeralda said. "Ultimately my emotional state of mind means nothing. What matters is that we can't keep dicking around with who's warm enough, and did we apply the right SPF for the mountain sun. Otherwise, this freaking mission will never end, and Lucy will turn forty and still not be married to Nicholas."

"I am not turning forty!" I glared at her.

"You'd better hope that you turn forty some day. What are your other options? Die young, beautiful, and tragic like James Dean or Marilyn Monroe? I'd prefer to turn forty, or fifty for that matter."

"I want to rock it at eighty," Zola said.

"We could be the giggle girls in our eighties," I said. "Royal Nana and Edith still have plenty of fun."

"When they're not fighting. Here, here!" Joan said. She pulled the silver flask of Prince Harry's scotch from her coat, unscrewed the top, downed a shot, and passed the flask around.

I shivered from another blast of frigid air, and gazed up at the steep incline in front of us. The snow appeared powdery, not too slick, due to a fresh six inches in a snowfall the night before. But that didn't negate the fact that I was standing in front of a substantial mountain peppered with black and blue diamond warning signs. While I might be able to navigate the bunny hill at Devil's Head in Wisconsin, these slopes appeared more formidable.

And then there was my fear of heights. You'd think all the airplane travel I'd undertaken in the past eighteen months, as well as the mile high sex, would have knocked that out of a girl. Unfortunately, nothing really knocked it out of a girl although Nick and I both really tried. "Perhaps I should let you expert skiers enjoy this spectacular adventure and I'll wait for you down there." I pointed to the boutique, cushy ski chalet down the hill.

"We're cross country skiing. Not down hill," Esmeralda said. "It's not that big of a deal. Milton Mertz told you he was here. We're going to find him and get that document signed."

"You mean get it signed again." I stared at the people standing in the line in front of us, waiting their turn on the chair lift. They leaned back, as the motorized bench scooped them up, their skis dangling below them as they were trundled up the very steep mountain. "Maybe we can track down Milton's number, text him, and meet him back at the lodge—"

"No more excuses," Esmeralda said, glancing back at the lift at the same moment it hit my butt hard, hoisting me in the air with all the dignity of a determined toddler grabbing a Tonka toy.

"Crap, that's going to bruise." I rubbed my behind. "My ass is going to look like an heirloom tomato by the time I get back to Fredonia." I held onto the ski lift's safety bar with my double insulated mittens for dear life as we rode uphill.

Yes, I had a fear of heights. Yes, my fingertips turned blue-ish white when the temps sunk under fifty degrees Fahrenheit. But I would get my signed document from the good Father, or whatever the heck he was, that certified I was unwed. I would get it here and now on this mountain if I had to take up yodeling to do it.

I glanced at Esmeralda who was in the seat on the lift next to me. *Her* ears weren't up to her shoulders. *She* wasn't gripping the bar like a desperate woman in the North Atlantic Ocean waters holding onto the edge of a Titanic lifeboat, screaming for someone to pull her into a rowboat. As always, Esmeralda appeared calm and collected: a rock, a port in a storm, the female Winston Churchill figure of our girl posse. It dawned on me that if I clung to the arm of her substantial ski parka, I might make it to the top of this mountain in one piece. I snuck my pink ski glove in her direction...

"Don't even think about it," she said.

"Why not?'

"Because it's past time that you conquered your fear of heights." She kicked her skis back and forth, causing our carriage to rock even more precariously.

"Now isn't a fair time to have that conversation." I sank back into the chair's cold metal bones. "It should be perfectly obvious I'm already doing that. One: We're in the Dolomite mountains. Not the flatlands. Two: We drove for hours up a twisty road with at least one thousand switchbacks, one of which I thought we wouldn't survive."

"You mean the one where the back end of the car slipped off the cliff, and Joan screamed, 'We're all going to die! We're all going to die!'?"

"Yes. Three: I'm on this stupid lift traveling up a steep

mountain even though I'm a horrible skier."

"But you survived," she said. "And look at all the tests you've passed the last few years. You, Lucy Trabbicio are a woman of honor. A woman of substance. A chick who just gets shit done. I've decided to tell you something I haven't told any of the ladies. But first I must swear you to secrecy."

"Fine." I glanced down at the tall pine trees that now appeared spindly from our vertically challenged perspective as the cold mountain breeze gusted.

"Hold up your right hand," she said.

"No. I'm holding onto the safety bar."

"I can't tell you my secret if you don't hold up your right hand."

"Can't you just take my word for it that I won't tell anybody?"

"No. I need you to solemnly swear on something very important, something sacred. You don't even have to tell me what it is, simply that you won't share with anyone what I'm about to tell you."

"Fine. But let's do this quick, 'K?" I held my pink mitten-clad hand in the air.

"Repeat after me: I, Lucille Marie Trabbicio."

"I, Lucille Marie Trabbicio," I said, peering at the exit platform that was quickly approaching. Holy crap, I had no idea how to ski off of one of these lifts. What if I fell in a heap as soon as we landed? What if the seat conked me on my head and I was knocked out, yet again? What if—

Esmeralda snapped her fingers in front of me. "Earth to Lucy."

"Yes, Yes."

"Repeat after me. I, Lucille Marie Trabbicio do solemnly swear that I will never, on pain of death, reveal what Lady Esmeralda Ilona Castile von Hapsburg is about to tell me."

"I, Lucy, do solemnly swear that I will never, blah blah

reveal with Lady Esmeralda blah blah is about to—oh holy crap we are landing and I have no idea how to do this."

"What do you mean you don't know how to land?"

"I've only skied down bunny slopes before," I said, hyperventilating.

"Get out of town."

"I wish I could."

"Deep breath. It's not as scary as it looks." Esmeralda reached out and patted my arm. "When the chair lift lowers, there will be several comfortable seconds for us to drop our skis onto the landing. Then we simply lean forward, push off with our skies—preferably to one side—and clear the way for persons arriving on the chair behind us. Got it?"

"Got it."

"Follow my lead. Here we go. On the count of three. One. Two. Three." She eased onto the landing and pushed off onto the sidelines.

I froze.

The chair rotated, turned around the bend, and unfortunately I was still on it.

"This is not the plan, Lucy," Esmeralda hollered, as Joan and Zola successfully exited the chair behind us and joined her.

"Fuck the plan," I said.

"Jump," Joan said. "Before it's too late!"

"I'm scared!"

"Do you want to be a Duchess of Fredonia?" Esmeralda asked.

"I could care less about titles." The distance between my skis and the snow covered hill increased.

"Do you want to marry Nicholas?" Zola asked.

"Marriage is provincial. I could live with him for a while."

"Do you want to see the Pinterest board we made for you with the mockups of your future children?" Joan asked.

"Yes!"

"Then you have to jump," Esmeralda hollered. "Push off, keep your knees slightly bent, tuck in your core. Everything will be fine."

I gazed down at the ground. It really wasn't all that far away. I closed my eyes. I let go. And I jumped.

I hit with a jolt but to my surprise I landed upright. I gazed over my shoulder at my ladies. "I did it!" I shook one ski pole triumphantly in the air. "I survived the ski lift landing. I, Lucy Marie whatever-my-last-name-is can totally do this skiing thing!"

"Lucy?" A man said.

He was clad in ski attire: tall, blonde, muscular with chiseled cheekbones, sporting reflective ski goggles. He was quite handsome actually, and looked familiar.

"Lucy?" He asked again.

"Yes," I said, right before I plowed into him, knocking him to the ground. We tumbled, falling like Jack and Jill down the hill, ending up in a pile in a powdery snow bank, our arms and legs entangled.

He lay on top of me, locks of wavy blonde hair splayed across my chest, his face planted firmly on my right boob, his legs pinned across mine. I probably could have squirmed out from beneath him, but quite frankly, all the wind was knocked out of me at this point, and it was all I could do to suck in air. "Sorry," I whispered. "So very sorry. I owe you a drink or perhaps a massage. You mentioned my name. Do we know each other?"

"Yes," he said, lifting his head and looking up at me. His lips full, his cheekbones sharp, his eyes hazel. "We walked down the aisle once, but you abandoned me for my brother."

"Oh crap. What are you doing here, Cristoph?"

CHAPTER 16

Thick flakes dropped from the dark, cloudy skies, quickly covering the trail in front of us. HRH Cristoph Edward George Timmel the Third, the crown prince of Fredonia, the ladies, and I, trekked along the path in a thickly wooded area as I munched on a chocolate bar.

"Nick kept texting me saying I needed to fly to Italy to protect you after your spill into the canal," Cristoph said. "He was relentless."

"How did he find out about that?"

"Mr. Philip Philips called Royal Nana and shared the whole story. Obviously she spoke with Nick. She too wants me here to help you track down Milton Mertz and get that affidavit signed."

"Is that why we detoured onto this trail?" I asked. We'd left behind the smooth slopes enjoyed by the downhill skiers. Now we ventured across steeper hills with sharp cliffs split by deep ravines crisscrossed by fallen trees and mountain streams at the bottom encrusted with ice.

"Yes. We're headed toward The Society's compound." He glanced over his shoulder again.

I couldn't help but wonder if something super fun was happening behind us. But when I peeked back the only thing I spotted was the ladies Esmeralda, Joan, and Zola following us on their skis.

"It is so nice of you to bring refreshments, Cristoph," I said. "After all the stress I've been under, the Friedricksburg chocolate bar really hits the spot. I'm not dieting anymore, you know. I gave that up after my last wedding."

"A pox on dieting. Nick doesn't care if you're up a stone or down," he said, glancing over his shoulder, again. "He just wants you safe and sound."

"Am I missing something happening back there?"

"No. Who's the new lady?"

"Zola Montbeliard."

"I don't recall seeing her at events or on the circuit. What do you know about her?"

"She's an art historian of sorts and friends with Esmeralda. I think she knows Nick."

"How does she know Nick and not me? That's practically impossible considering the circles we run in."

"You need to ask Nick that," I said, glancing back over my shoulder and catching her staring at Cristoph, "Or better yet—Zola."

"No time. I'm here to help you. Look over that ridge, up toward the right. Do you see that cluster of modern buildings in the near distance?"

"The ones surrounded by barbed wire fence and a guard hut at the front gate?"

"Yes. Nana's people have ascertained that it's been leased by the Society of Royal Alchemists. It's a retreat, or commune of sorts where Milton Mertz has taken refuge with like-minded cohorts."

"That sounds so mysterious."

He shrugged, took off his ski cap, shook the snow from it, and then shoved it back in his pocket. "Not my circus, not my monkeys. You and Nicholas, however, are under my care. Speaking of which—you have two inches of snow on your head and you look like a snow cone." He leaned forward and brushed the snow off my woolen cap. "After your dive into the Venice canal, you don't want to come down with a common cold. Did you really take the plunge to save Nick's texts?"

"No. Kind of. Perhaps I slipped. Okay, yes." I copped to my humiliation, paused, and dusted off snow from my legs. "Seriously, why are you here?

He stopped in his tracks, grabbed a water bottle from his knapsack and held it out to me.

"I'm good, thanks."

He slugged back a drink. "Nana knows Mr. Philips threw out his back again and thought you might need some help. According to her advisors the affidavit is your legal loophole out of this mess. She wants this whole thing done and put to bed."

"Of course we're getting this done." Esmeralda approached with Joan and Zola. "Nice of you to show up late to the party. Do you have any more of those chocolate bars?"

"Better late than never." He dug through his knapsack, grabbed a handful, and passed them to the ladies.

It was then I saw a familiar figure far behind the barbed wire fence on a large open expanse. The man wore a thick parka and snow boots, sported a ruddy face, and waved a green day-glow Frisbee high in the air. A Black Labrador retriever and an enormous tri-colored Bernese Mountain Dog barked up at him, wagging their tails.

I suddenly missed my beloved Tulip.

"Who's taking care of my dog?"

"Mom," Cristoph said. "By the time you return she'll be even more of a princess if that's possible."

I smiled. If we weren't on a mission, I'd be half tempted to run to the fence, throw myself over it, and ask if I too could be included in the game. The man threw the Frisbee, and I caught a full frontal glimpse of his face. I inhaled sharply as my hand flew to my chest. "It's Milton Mertz," I said. "Oh my God, what are the odds?"

Esmeralda whipped out a pair of binoculars and peered through them. "It is Milton Mertz, poser."

Joan grabbed the binoculars from her and stared through them. "He's behind a barb wired fence with two armed guards patrolling the inside perimeter."

"What's the big deal?" I asked. "He already gave me his signature once. I'm sure if I just walk up to the gate, call out to him super nice, he'll give his John Hancock to me again. Who has a copy of the affidavit we need signed?"

"I do," Cristoph and the ladies said in unison.

"Everyone but me?"

"We didn't want to burden you with more worries," Esmeralda said. "Lucy, you don't know if the poser is accessible, let alone friendly. We're in the middle of a deserted forest, a decent hike away from any popular ski trails. That compound does not look warm and fuzzy."

I frowned. "There are dogs."

"The guard has an Uzzi," Esmeralda said.

"The Society of Royal Alchemists is very old," Zola said. "They have secrets and rules that we are not privy to. Milton Mertz might be in seclusion. He might not even be allowed to meet with you face to face, let alone give you another signature on the affidavit."

"Let's not forget I'm a barrister," Joan said. "If we can't get his signature on the affidavit, we can pursue other legal action to force him to right his wrong."

I shook my head. "Technically it's not his 'wrong' at this point. It's mine. I'm the one who fell in the water after he signed the document. It's basically my fault at this stage in the game that we're even here, trekking about in the cold snow, eating chocolate. I'm enormously sorry. You've all taken time out of your busy lives to help me with my dilemma, and I appreciate it enormously. If I hadn't fallen in the stupid canal in Venice we'd be back in Sauerhausen right now, enjoying some Christmas cheer, drinking spiked eggnog, exchanging gifts, and doing last minute shopping." Tears trickled out of the corners of my eyes and I felt like a pathetic, monumental loser. "I apologize for ruining your Christmases," I sniffled.

"Well I for one am sorry-not sorry," Esmeralda said. "I got laid by the hot Italian chauffeur. He was exceptional in the sack. I got his digits. Christmas came a little early this year if you know what I mean. Happy Holidays."

"I'm sorry-not sorry," Joan said. "I scored an excellent ball gown and went from wallflower to blooming bud in Venice of all places. Gareth's visiting me in Sauerhausen for New Years Eve. Happy Holidays, my friends!"

"I'm sorry-not sorry," Cristoph said as he and Zola locked eyes. "Can I buy you a hot cocoa Lady Montbeliard with Baileys when we get back to civilization?"

"Yes," Zola said. "I'm sorry-not sorry. I am having more fun with you all than I've had with my head in the history books for the past six months."

Joan wrapped her arm around me and gave me a quick hug. "So you see, Lucy, our Christmases are turning out just fine in spite of your dilemma. How about yours?"

I missed Nicholas. I missed his face. I missed his voice. I missed our time together. All I wanted for Christmas was to be officially married to my Nick. I turned and stared at Milton Mertz playing Frisbee with the dogs romping through the snow behind the barbed wire fence manned by the guards. He still held the key to my happiness.

Or did he?

Maybe I held the key to my happiness.

What if I had been looking to someone else for permission or the ability to solve my problems when the entire time, I was the person in charge of solving my own problems? I was my own champion.

I was my own knightress in shining fucking armor.

I gazed at Milton Mertz through the snow falling more heavily around us, obscuring my vision. But I could still see one thing clearly: exercise time with the dogs was over. He turned and headed back toward the large compound further into the depths of the property, the pooches following reluctantly behind him as they tugged on the either side of the Frisbee.

"It's okay, Lucy," Joan said. "It's past time to turn back. The weather is inclement. We'll sit in front of a toasty fireplace, have a drink, and figure out a legal plan of attack. Yes, it will be a slower approach. It will probably take a few years, but eventually you and Nicholas could wed again."

"No!" I unlatched my skis and kicked them to the side. "I am getting this done and I am getting it done now." I clapped my pink mittens together, and raced forward as fast as a woman resembling a round pastel pastry could run through snowy mountain terrain. "Father McGillicuddy!" I hollered.

He paused mid-stride, as the dogs looked around.

I skirted around a fallen tree bumping out onto the path.

"Hang on, Lucy!" Cristoph said. "I'll do this."

"Milton Mertz! Please stop! Don't go inside!" I kept running, the barbed wire fence growing closer in my sight. The snow pounding dull under my boots. The path narrowed. I was closer to steep drop-offs, but I didn't care. The heavens opened up and the snow beat down thicker around me with a fury.

"Lucy, for God's sakes, stop!" Esmeralda yelled. "I'm connected. If push comes to shove, I can call in favors. I have ways to track this poser down. It's part of the secret I was trying to tell you on the chairlift."

"Father McGillicuddy!" I said. "Wait!"

He peered at me as the dogs raced toward the fence, bounding through the snow, barking excitedly. "Lucy?"

"Yes!" I paused to catch my breath and waved at him. "Yes! I have one more favor to ask. Could you sign that affidavit one last time? There was a problem with the last one."

"Of course, Lucy," He waved at the guards, "Let her in the gate."

"Thank you! Thank you so very much!" I looked back at the ladies and Cristoph. "You see what I mean? That wasn't all that tough." I moved forward on the narrow path, stepping onto a thick tree trunk covered in snow. I heard a crisp crunch as my foot fell through the rotted wood and I tumbled down the cliff into a ravine.

❧

Cristoph, the ladies, Milton Mertz, and a few of his pals tried to rescue me after I tumbled down the treacherous ravine but quickly came to the conclusion that this course of action would lead to all of us being trapped and freezing to death.

Instead, Milton alerted the secretary at the Society of Royal Alchemists lodge who called the Air and Rescue Unit. They'd flown a chopper in over the mountains, as Nick and a few of the guardsmen extricated me from the snowy crevasse in the Dolomites Mountains.

And wonder of all wonders, my Nicholas was dispatched

down the ladder to get me out of here. "Jesus, Lucy," he said as he rappelled down into the gorge and raced to my side. "Are you okay? Are you all right?"

"Everything feels okay except for my ankle. And I'm cold. Oh my God, I can't believe you're here!"

"I'm sorry, my love." He grabbed a thermal blanket from his backpack and wrapped it around me. "I don't want you to keep doing dangerous things. We need to have a talk about this."

"Yes, sir, soldier." I saluted him. "You look pretty hot in a uniform. Hey—nice ass. Do you work out? I'm sorry! That's the trauma talking."

He kissed me thoroughly, and then got down to business.

No, not that kind of business. It was too cold outside and I'd been in this gorge for over an hour. He strapped me into a cot attached to thick ropes. "Shut your eyes and breathe," he said, kissing me once on the lips, then signaling with his walkie-talkie. The rescue team hauled me out of the valley up toward the helicopter.

It dawned on me as I swayed through the air high above the ground, that as much as I thought I could do everything myself, it helped to have bitchin BFFs, a hot fiancé with guard training, and a future brother-in-law who'd finally procured the signed affidavit from Milton Mertz, aka Father McGillicuddy.

Yes, the document was signed, in the proper hands, and it seems my marital nightmare was coming to an end.

Nick cradled me in his arms in the back of the Air Vac helicopter, as thick 'Whop-Whop-Whop' sounds emanated from the blades slicing through chilly air as we flew high over the Alps.

"I can't believe you're none the worse for wear." He kissed my forehead and examined my face, again, for cuts and bruises, while I examined his for sheer deliciousness.

"Except for a sprained ankle," the paramedic said, placing the boot he'd sliced off my foot to the side and wrapping my ankle with compression tape.

"I missed you so very much," Nick said. "You need to stop going out on a limb to get everything done."

"It wasn't a limb. It was a log on a cliff. And who knew that tree trunk was rotted out? No one could have predicted that."

"Probably anyone who's tromped around a forest could have predicted that."

"Clearly I grew up in Chicago and don't know a lot about forests. You've got to give me a pass on that one."

I told Nick to dispatch Cristoph and the ladies. He arranged for the ski resort to send an ATV to transport them back to the lodge. They could get warmed up while while Nick and I visited the Cortina d'Ampresszo Urgent Care Facility, a small, but top- notch medical center. Being that this town was a mecca for winter sports, the medical staff had seen more than their fair share of broken bones and sprained ankles, and knew their way around ice packs and an X-ray machine.

A few hours later I declined the wheelchair, and exited the facility wearing a mid-calf orthopedic boot and walking with the help of my new crutches to the snow-covered parking lot. A driver flashed the lights on a waiting SUV, its engine running. "Where are Cristoph and the ladies?" I asked.

"Hanging out at the Aprè Ski Party in town," Nick said. "Do you want to join them?"

I shook my head, smiled, and limped toward the vehicle. "Correct me if I'm wrong, but I suspect you're only on a brief leave, solider. You'll have to return to active duty shortly."

"True, my lady." He placed a protective hand on my waist.

I paused to shift my balance to maneuver into the back of the SUV. I stared up into his handsome blue eyes rimmed with dark lustrous eyelashes, reached out and traced the cleft in his chin with my index finger. "I'm single now, you know. I was thinking about ways to thank you properly. Does anything come to mind?" I batted my eyelashes and bit my lower lip.

"Yes." He pulled me flush against him, and kissed me long and slow, his tongue teasing my lips open, exploring, tempting, claiming. He pulled back, gazed into my eyes, smiled, and tucked a lock of hair behind my ear. "Remember that ring I gave you back at our townhouse in Sauerhausen? The pretty one with the rather large diamond?"

"Yes," I said.

"I want to slide it on your ring finger tomorrow, Lucy. Right after I marry you."

I smiled. "I can live with that. But what will we do between tonight and tomorrow?"

"We'll come up with something."

CHAPTER 17

We were married the next evening in a candlelight ceremony on the outdoor deck of the lodge. I wore a long sleeved, warm-fitted white with silver flecked brocade gown with a faux fur trimmed hood. Gareth Trent had already made it for a winter fashion show. He drove it up the mountain himself and fitted it to me at the last minute.

It was a small, intimate ceremony. Royal Nana, King Frederick and Queen Cheree flew in early afternoon. Considering this was the fourth time I was marrying one of the King's sons, I suspected he wanted to bail, but Queen Cheree had probably twisted his arm to put in an appearance.

I put Lady Esmeralda in charge of videoing the event for my pal Alida and my Uncle John back in Chicago. I asked Lady Zola to Facetime Lady Cheryl who was still enjoying the holidays in Crete with her family.

"Do you think you can walk down this aisle?" Joan asked, as she dabbed on my lipstick, blotted it, and adjusted my decorative hood over my hair that had been styled to cascade down my shoulders.

"Yes. Besides, I have to. Royal Nana and Edith decorated my crutches."

We glanced at them. Silk ribbons in the royal Fredonia colors: purple, gold, and white were wrapped around them; lush white rose corsages discretely attached onto the handlebars.

"Festive," Joan said, coughing into her hand.

I sighed. I'd forgiven Father Florentine for being the bearer of bad news only because Royal Nana insisted that a church-approved priest conduct the ceremony. He was the only officiant we could procure during the Christmas holidays at such late notice.

Now Nick and Cristoph stood at the far end of the deck, both dressed in black tuxes with white shirts and black bowties, candlelight flickering over them. Dear God, they were handsome—Queen Cheree's Irish twins.

But my Nicholas was my keeper. My Nicholas was my love. The man who'd captured my heart for an eternity.

Mr. Philips did me the honors, and walked me down the very short aisle. Or, should I say, helped me hobble. I knew this marriage would be the keeper. The one that sealed the deal. I looked up into Nicholas's blue eyes. He looked so handsome as he beckoned to me with his index finger. "You're mine, Lucy."

I smiled at him. "I'm yours, Nicholas."

And so a handsome prince promised a klutzy commoner for the third time to love, honor, protect, and keep her as his wife. I promised as well, and we sealed the deal under a clear winter sky, the stars sparkling in the dark heavens above us, as he slid that gorgeous ring on my finger, and kissed me.

"I love you, Lucy," he said. "I'll always love you."

I couldn't help but think that I was the luckiest girl in the world. I'd finally gotten everything I wanted for Christmas. Because all I ever wanted was Nicholas.

N ick and I rang in the New Year back at our new townhouse in Sauerhausen. Thick snow fell outside the two-story floor –to-ceiling windows as lights twinkled in the city's background.

"Your new husband, has a 'Welcome to your new official home' surprise present for you in his pants pockets," Nick said. "Don't you want to know what he got you?"

"As long as it's not another silver place setting, I'll be happy."

"You're going to be very happy." Nick captured my hand in his, raised it to his lips, and kissed it. "I love you, Lucy."

"I love you too, Nick. I'm sorry I'm so crabby. My fingers are cramping from writing all the thank you notes." I moved my hand down his firm, broad chest, and caressed his hard stomach with the six pack abs. "Writing original material isn't all that easy you know. I think about every word I write and I personalize every note. I know that's probably old fashioned, but perhaps in this hashtag world too often filled with posers, charlatans, and short-cuts— maybe that means something. Maybe it shows I'm for real. Maybe it shows I care."

"I know you care, baby," Nick said, his breath hitching.

"Good." I smiled. The further south I travelled, hello, I'd pretty much figured out what the surprise was. "Tell HRH I miss him." I ran my hand lightly over his jeans as HRH saluted and waved the royal Fredonia flag in my honor. "And that I'll be visiting soon. We will have détente if it's the last thing I do. 'Stronger Together!' I heard that somewhere recently."

"If it's the last thing you do in the next five minutes, you mean," he said. "HRH is sending you an imperial edict, Lucy. Perhaps to keep the politicians happy, we should have a royal quickie? I missed our new pudding couch. We bought it because it was sturdy, right?" He sat down and slapped his hand on the cushions. "Firm. Solid."

"What politicians?" I couldn't help but smile.

"Oh, you know, those old windbags. The diehards. The ones that take the floor and talk for hours and make people's ears bleed. Our new sofa begs to be re-christened now that we are officially married. In fact, I hear it calling my name." He put a hand to his ear. "What is that I hear, pudding couch? Oh, you think Lucy should stop worrying about matters that will resolve themselves and we should spend our time and energy breaking in the new place? Yes, pudding couch. I am a good husband. Of course I will relay that message."

My heart cracked open, and I realized how very much I loved being married to this delicious man. I walked toward him, straddled him, and wrapped my arms around his neck.

"Hello," he said.

"Hello." I unzipped his jeans and reached for the prize inside. "I don't think you need these pants. These pants need to disappear."

"The pants thought you'd never ask." He yanked them off.

There was a loud 'Knock-Knock-Knock' on our front door.

"Are you expecting guests?" I asked.

"No. Ignore that. It's probably the pizza delivery guy getting my address mixed up with Cristoph's again. Jeez, we live right next door. It should be perfectly obvious we are the pepperoni people and he is the sausage and mushroom guy."

"Right," I said, and resumed nibbling on his neck.

Three knocks sounded again on our door.

"Crap!" Nick said, squirming out from underneath me, and pulling on his jeans. He strode to the entrance, peered through the peephole, and flung the door open. "Do I know you?" he asked the man in the priestly robes with the prune-faced mouth who swept into our townhouse like a breath of stale air.

"Of course you know me," he sniffed. "I baptized you. I'm Archbishop Causesdesperdues."

"Aha. Yes, well it's been a while. So nice of you to visit us," Nick said. "Perhaps you could have called us first."

"But, I'm not here on a mission of the heart, Prince Nicholas. I'm here on palace business." He turned to his guards and pointed at Nick. "Arrest this man!"

My eyes nearly popped out of my head as I watched three thugs in military uniforms handcuff my Nicholas. "What the hell are you doing?" I pushed myself off the couch and ran to him.

"Anyone who has sexual relations with the Prince of Fredonia's wife is subject to arrest and imprisonment," Archbishop Causesdesperdues said.

"What the hell are you talking about?" I asked, glaring at them. "I'm married to the Prince of Fredonia, you big numnut. Unshackle my husband, immediately!"

"Indeed you are married to the Prince of Fredonia," he said. "According to the paperwork that was filed with the church and the state on December 20th in this year of our Lord, you, Lucille, married HRH Cristoph Edward George Timmel the Third, the crown prince of Fredonia. Take this man to the dungeons!"

"What?" I asked.

"What?" Nick asked as the guards dragged him away.

"The paperwork is clear. I even went out of my way to make you a copy. According to the documents filed, you, Lucille Marie Trabbicio are lawfully married to HRH Cristoph Edward George Timmel the Third. So sorry to disturb you, Duchess," Archbishop Causesdesperdues said. "Happy New Year."

"What the hell? You're married to my brother?" Nick asked as they pulled him out of our townhouse.

"It's not possible. Clearly there's been a mistake. I married you. We have pictures," I said. We put them on Facebook."

"You can't trust social media." Archbishop Causesdesperdues sniffed.

"*All Right Magazine* purchased our official wedding pictures. The proceeds went to charity."

"It's fake news," he said, gesticulating with his fat little fingers.

"I have a Pinterest board with mock-up pictures of our future children!"

"Check the paperwork. It's all in order. Happy New Year!" Archbishop Causesdesperdues pulled his cape tighter over his stumpy body and stomped out of our townhouse.

"You're married to Cristoph?" Nick asked as the guards hustled him into the courtyard. "Good God, what are we going to do now?"

"I don't know." I raked my fingers through my hair. "I'll figure out something. We'll figure out something. We always do..."

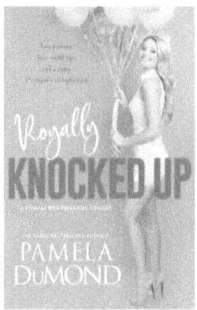

Dear Reader: Thanks so much for reading POSER! I hope you love Lucy and Nick's romance and enjoy the Ladies-in-Waiting adventures. Lucy will get her Happily Ever After in Royally Knocked Up #4. But will she be wed to Crown Prince Cristoph or his younger brother Nick?

"Pamela's **books are like potato chips,** you cannot read just one..."~

Jenny James One click Royally Knocked Up #4 now! Or turn the page to read an excerpt.

Sign up for my NEWSLETTER to get release info, news on sales, upcoming books, games, etc.

Looking for a hilarious matchmaking Romantic Comedy with backstory that has the feels? You'll love Ms. Match Meets a Millionaire ! Turn the page to read an excerpt.

Sign up for my NEWSLETTER to get release info, news on sales, upcoming books, games, etc. Like my Pamela DuMond Author page. Join my private reading group Pamela DuMond's Dirty Darlings.

Happy reading!

Pamela DuMond

EXCERPT OF ROYALLY
KNOCKED UP

DESCRIPTION

I'm a former cocktail waitress, an American commoner, a chick who fell in love with and royally wed Prince Nicholas of Fredonia.

How the hell did I end up married to his brother Crown Prince Cristoph?

Marrying into the Fredonia royal family is about as uneventful as walking through a dog park barefoot and blind-folded after the snow melts.

Has Cristoph carried a torch for me ever since I left him high and dry at the cathedral's altar?

Did Cristoph sabotage my marriage to Nick?

Am I hallucinating or did the stick really turn blue?

PRAISE

Five Stars "...peppered with **adult humor** and swoon worthymoments..." A. Reviewer

One click Royally Knocked Up #4 now!

Chapter 1

I shivered, pulled the sash of my warm, woolen coat tighter around me, and glanced around Old Town, a neighborhood of Sauerhausen, the capital city of Fredonia. I adjusted the scarf that I'd been wearing for over forty-eight straight hours and brushed off a few donut crumbs. I'd already dribbled a mochaccino down my front and the smell of buttermilk curdled crème mingled with the bitter fragrance of smashed dreams. It was a cold, crappy morning in hell and I wasn't all that happy about it.

I usually adored this bustling European metropolis: its energy, the friendly hustle-bustle vibe, and its architecture -- a mish-mash of modern structures made of concrete block and glass, juxtaposed with gorgeous older buildings that resembled decadent pastel colored pastries. The jail that my kind-of-husband was being held in, fell in the former category. I stared at it now, standing in front of it, knowing my beloved Nicholas was just behind its walls. It looked like sad wedding cake that had been left out of the box for too long, icicles dripping from its roof.

Perhaps I was projecting my own insecurities and simply describing myself. I was a hot mess: makeup-less, sleepless, groom-less. Oh. Skip that one, because apparently there was a possibility that I *was* married, just not to the right guy. More specifically, not to the right *brother*.

I had signed up to marry Prince Nicholas Frederick of Fredonia, he of the wavy jet black hair, come hither blue eyes, and six pack abs so ripped I massaged my hands against them every night. I had signed up, on numerous occasions might I add, to marry this delicious man with the hilarious sense of humor. He was the younger prince of Fredonia, the 'spare' to the throne, but I didn't give a rat's ass about royal titles and monarchy, pomp and privilege. I did, however, care very much about Nicholas.

I cared about the thoughts in Nick's brain, and every inch of his delectable body. I cared about his kindness, the way he treated people, myself included, with honor and dignity. I cared that he loved me so much he'd married me three, *count that*, three times now. Which is why it pained me that through some cruel twist of fate, I was now quite possibly legally wed to his older brother, Cristoph. Oh yes, a few days after my last royal wedding, Archbishop Causesdesperdues had butted into my life again, insisting that I was married to the *other* prince of Fredonia.

What's the problem, Lucy, one might ask? Cristoph was equally hot, the heir to Fredonia's throne, the handsome blonde playboy crown prince who had slept with half of the eligible ladies in Europe, and was tackling other continents as well.

While I'd never had sex with Cristoph—we'd made out a once or twice in the past—purely in the line of my former part-time job. And yes, I knew his attractions were... sizeable. But my brother-in-law's charms were the least of my worries because my Nicholas was still incarcerated, and this pained me.

I glanced at the royal Sauerhausen prison that was in serious need of a paint job, but acted like it didn't care, squatting imperiously behind high, thick, wrought iron fences. Palace guards wearing warm winter coats accented in the royal colors of purple, white, and gold stomped up and down the perimeters, trying not to shiver in the gloomy cold.

It was January 2, and the skies were gray with approaching storm clouds. It had been two days since my Nicholas had been taken into custody and thrown into jail by Archbishop Causesdesperdues and his bullies. Or as I liked to call him, Archbishop Asshat. Two days and two nights that my husband—maybe *technically* not my husband, but whatever, *should* have been my husband—had been forcibly removed from our home and ripped away from me.

After Asshat's guards cuffed Nick, they escorted, or should I say—bullied—him away from our home, and stuffed him into the back seat of a black, shiny town car. I chased after them imploring them to release him. Okay, fine. I swore like a sailor while flipping them off with both hands, but they ignored me as the sedan peeled off, smoke belching from the tailpipe.

I raced after them, absolutely livid, until I couldn't run any longer. I stopped, hunching over to catch my breath. I felt hopeless and helpless, but then realized what needed to happen: I rallied my ladies-in-waiting.

We texted, phoned, face-timed, messengered, and e-mailed. The ladies called their friends who called *their* friends, and now I, together with a few hundred women were marching in a sisterhood of protest outside the cakebread jail, carrying picket signs proclaiming: "Release Prince Nicholas!" "False Arrest!" "Down with the Fake-riarchy!" as we chanted, "Hell no, we won't go!"

"Lucy. Speaking of hell, you look just like it." Lady Joan Brady tugged on my arm, pulling me out of the crowd of protestors onto the sidelines. "Why don't we take a quick break? It will do us both good." She pulled a thermos from her Gareth Trent designer tote and unscrewed the top.

"I hope that's the really extra strong super black coffee." I rubbed my hands together, pressed them to my mouth and blew on them.

"Triple dark French blend for you, my friend." She poured two cups of steaming brew and handed one to me. "It'll zap you awake quicker than a cattle prod and bonus—it warms the hands. You've been out here since the night Nick was arrested. You need some sleep, a warm bed, and as much as I love you, trust me on this, you need to shower."

I held up one arm, sniffed my armpit, and cringed. "Was Joan of Arc all that worried about her hygiene when leading French troops into war with the English?"

"My namesake only had the locals following her. If the paparazzi had been hounding Joan it would have been a different story. She might have practiced her key talking points and polished her armor. Maybe it's time you return to the townhouse and regroup. Let the palace lawyers and the bureaucrats figure this out."

"And leave Nick all by himself inside a jail cell at the beginning of the New Year? At the start of our marriage?" I frowned. "That would be a shitty thing to do to him, let alone set a terrible example of the kind of wife I aspire to be. I will *not* be the woman who's only there for her husband during the good times. I didn't enter this marriage for titles or headlines and trust me, he didn't either."

"I know, Lucy." Lady Esmeralda Castile von Haspburgh joined us, elbowing into our tiny huddle. She held out her mug. "Caffeinate me, Joanie not of Arc."

She did, and Esmeralda sipped from her steaming cup. "My sources, Lucy, tell me now that if you're wed to Cristoph, you'll have moved up five places in the line to become Queen of Fredonia some day."

"I couldn't care less about becoming the queen of

anything." I gazed at the prison, wondering if Nick could see me through one of the windows from his cell, possibly on the second or third floor. On the off chance, I waved and then blew him a kiss.

"That's not true," Joan said. "Everyone wants to become queen of something."

"Fine. You're right," I said. "I claim pizza. I'd like to become Queen of pizza some day. Thin crust, pepperoni with mushrooms. And for the last time, Esmeralda, you might think you know everything but you don't. I'm *not* married to Cristoph!"

"Archbishop Causesdesperdues says you are."

"Archbishop Causesdesperdues has his head up his ample, floppy behind. You were at my wedding. You listened to me pledge my trout—"

"Your troth."

"My trout, my troth..." My temper flared. I grabbed Esmeralda by the shoulders of her double-breasted crimson woolen winter coat and shook her. "Whatever the fish, or the promise, I pledged it to Nicholas. NOT Cristoph!"

I heard a distinct crack, and it came from Esmeralda. She widened her eyes.

"Oh my God! I'm so sorry! I was somewhat violent with you. Are you all right?"

"I'm fabulous. You just adjusted my middle back better than my chiropractor has done in years."

A firm hand landed on my shoulder. "Trouble, ladies?"

I whipped around and saw a familiar face. "Major Peters!" I stared at the handsome late thirty-something man in a military uniform.

"Actually, it's Captain Sam."

"Of course. Captain Sam. You helped us so much when Nick was kidnapped."

"I'll never forget our mission to Monaco," he said. "You

ladies were superb. Who knew you could harmonize like Diana Ross and the Supremes?"

"Technically we were the Ice Cream Dreams. That was crazy! It's been a few months since I've seen you, Captain Sam. What brings you back to Sauerhausen?"

"Oh, he knows what brought him to Sauerhausen," Esmeralda said. "And Captain Sam also knows why he should have stayed the hell away." She swiveled and walked off, her head high, her hips swinging from side to side.

"Aren't you going to say hi to Captain Sam?" I asked.

She waved at us dismissively.

"I don't understand. I know we are all stressed out. But why is Esmeralda being so rude?"

He cleared his throat. "Because I get under her skin."

"Pun intended?"

"Yes. Happy New Year to you, Duchess."

"I'm not a Duchess."

"That remains to be seen. Since last I've seen you, I've been given a promotion. I'm now personal attaché to the Prince of Fredonia. His go to person. The man assigned to help him with pressing palace matters, sticky situations, you know, the usual."

"That sounds terrific!" I said. "Congratulations. So, you'll be working for Nicholas and be able to help us track down what went wrong with this latest snafu. It's only been a couple of days, but I can't reach Cristoph. I think he's the guy to clear this whole thing up. I suspect he has a new woman in his life because he's not at his townhouse, and he's not answering any of my texts. He probably spirited his new lady off to a tropical island where they're surfing, sailing, fishing, enjoying sunsets to die for and inhaling their 5 star meals. They're frolicking naked in the Caribbean, or the Seychelles while I'm stuck here in Sauerhausen smelling like curdled milk and yesterday's dreams."

"Actually, Prince Cristoph is here," Captain Sam said. "He touched down at the airport a little over an hour ago and is making his way toward us, even as we speak. Look."

I glanced up and spotted the black, shiny Mercedes town car with two motorcycles driven by security police leading the way through the crowds.

"Thank God! Fredonia's playboy prince might be a wild child but he's no one's fool. He loves his family, and he's got a heart of gold. Tell me he's going to end this mess here and now? That he'll declare this is just a big, crazy mix up and that Nick and I are truly married? That there's been fake news about Fredonia royal marriages, and weddings."

"No," he said. "That's not going to happen."

"But he has to do something."

"Oh he is. Prince Cristoph is going to invoke an ancient royal law, break Nick out of this jail, and have him transported to the palace where he'll be under house arrest."

"That's terrific, I think." I smelled something a bit rank, and frowned upon realizing it was me. "I need to go home and shower before I drive to the palace to see Nick."

"There's plenty of time," he said. "But I believe you have to schedule your visit with the proper authorities in advance."

"Right. What is this ridiculousness with the whole house arrest thing? These adultery charges need to be dropped. Nick and I are legally wed. There is no way I'm married to Cristoph."

He sighed. "There's been a cock-up."

"What do you mean, a cock-up?"

"You know, a screw up, a mistake of epic proportions. The kind of thing that goes down in history books as being one of those quirky blunders that everyone loves to dissect, and tries to figure out where it all went wrong. But when all is said and done, it's tough to put a finger on it because a cock-up takes on a life of its own and becomes either a tragedy of comic proportions or a comedy with a tragic flare."

"This ordeal is some weird kind of misunderstanding and someday we'll laugh about it over a nice single malt Scotch," I said. "But right now I am sleep deprived, my skin is tingling, and it doesn't feel all that funny. I need to go home. Shower. Feed my dog and snuggle with her for a minute. And then visit my husband. I want to hug him, and kiss him, and tell him everything's going to be all right. That we can go back to our married life. Is that too much for a girl to ask? Is that too much for a new bride to ask about her new husband?"

Captain Sam stared at his feet. "Actually, no. That's one of the reasons I'm here. To escort you home."

"Thank God! 11211 Centralaski Park West, please."

"Actually I'll be driving you to 11213 Centralaski Park West."

"But that's Cristoph's place."

"And yours as well, Duchess. I'm here to escort you back to your royal residence as the lawfully married wife of Prince Cristoph of Fredonia, heir to the Fredonia throne."

One click Royally Knocked Up #4 now!

Royally Knocked Up Royally Wed Romantic Comedy#4

EXCERPT OF MS. MATCH MEETS A MILLIONAIRE

Ms. Match Meets a Millionaire

A PLAYING SWEETER ROMANTIC COMEDY

DESCRIPTION

A standalone Rom-Com from *USA Today* bestselling author Pamela DuMond.

I, Harper Emily Schubert, am an underpaid assistant working at a matchmaking agency, surviving on Insta-Ramen and dreams. How was it possible that I made a love match that resulted in the society marriage of the year?

Christmas season is upon us and I plan on enjoying this gorgeous wedding by drinking too much Champagne and relaxing for a change. I didn't plan on running into a gorgeous, tuxedo-clad brick wall of a man.

I didn't plan on him stopping my fall by grabbing onto my boob and *Not. Letting. Go.* I most definitely didn't plan on this impossibly handsome man being my new client.

Ethan's heir to the Rosseaux Hotel fortune, whip smart, hilariously funny, and so yummy. I'm tempted to... *good God I want to...* but dating clients is a big, fat 'No-No.'

Aren't some rules meant to be broken?

CHAPTER ONE

Harper

"Tradition insists, Mrs. Lesley Biltenhouse, that I remove your garter with my teeth."

The geeky- cute, middle-aged groom knelt and rested his chin on the bride's thigh. He gazed up at her, smitten. "Or our first year of married life will go to hell."

"You just made that up, John." Lesley smoothed her three-and-a-half carat diamond-encrusted hand across his shaggy salt and pepper hair, tucking a wayward lock behind his ear.

"But it sounded convincing." He grinned, dove back to her garter, snagged it between his teeth, and dragged it down her leg. The bride stifled her giggles and the black-tie wedding crowd erupted in laughter and enthusiastic applause.

I leaned back against the wall of the grand ballroom at the posh Rosseaux Hotel on the Magnificent Mile in downtown Chicago and applauded along with them. The skin on the back of my arms erupted in goosebumps.

Breathe, Harper. This is not a dress rehearsal. You made this happen. Breathe.

I smoothed my designer tea-length gown down my legs, the raw silk scratchy against my bare knees. Its prickly roughness grounded me in reality, which was good. I couldn't afford to be kidnapped by commercialism, swept away like a chick in one of those stupid commercials for Dead Sea bath salts. I had too much to get done, too much at stake.

I, Harper Emily Schubert, a woman whose income hovered slightly above the poverty line, was the person responsible for brokering the Biltenhouse marriage resulting in the swank, society Chicago wedding of the year. My bosses at the White Glove Matchmaking Agency had rewarded my efforts, promoting me from shlepper of coffee and water-er of plants to junior agent. I'd start my new position on Monday, but this weekend was mine all mine, and I planned on enjoying myself tonight.

I sipped the top-shelf Champagne and glanced around at all the gorgeousness an expensive, tasteful wedding offered. The Rosseaux Hotel was built in the 1920s, a throwback to elegance and old-fashioned glamour. The ballroom was decked out for the Christmas holidays: Italian lights twinkled, draped over wreathes hung on the wallpapered ballroom walls as well as the fifteen-foot Douglas fir in the corner, decorated with sparkling Tiffany ornaments. I inhaled the scent of pine needles and freshly-cut flower arrangements that intermingled with notes of expensive perfumes and colognes.

Heaven. I'd landed in heaven.

I tipped my head back and drained my glass of Champagne. The bubbles swirled into my bloodstream and my shoulders slid off my ears for the first time in the year since I'd moved to Chicago. I stretched my neck right to left, then side to side, and decided one more drink couldn't hurt. I swiveled to look for a waiter but collided boobs first into a tall, solid, brick wall of a man carrying a tray. "Oof!"

"Sorry," he said.

"*I'm* sorry!" My face was buried against his rock-hard chest and I spotted only a flash of muscular largeness, a hint of his black tux, and a glimpse of chiseled cheekbones as we mashed up against each other.

Oh no.

Oh, crappity-crap.

This would not do.

I'd leased my gown from Cinderella For a Night and had had my hair styled at the South Dearborn Beauty Academy. I needed to fit in with this crowd. These people were potential clients. I couldn't afford to be seen canoodling in public at this wedding. I leaned back on my heels, sucked in my core, and pulled a few inches away from the hot waiter.

My small movement pitched the hot waiter off balance. He bobbled the serving tray high in the air with one hand, and grabbed onto a large decanter with his other, saving it from falling. But a crystal tumbler filled with liquor seized the opportunity to break free and wobbled at the edge of the tray.

"Dammit!" I said, watching the glass plummet toward my cleavage.

"Dammit!" he said, his eyes widening as he abandoned the decanter and reached for the tumbler.

I sucked in my stomach. The glass skimmed past my chest and crashed onto the carpet, splashing thick amber liquor onto my legs and skirt at exactly the same time the hot waiter's hand landed squarely on my silken bodice, where it remained, large fingers firmly clamped on my boob. The feeling wasn't all that unpleasant.

I glared up at the guy ready to kill or dismember him, but his hazel eyes—or were they green—appeared remorseful, as did the set of his jaw, and the pout of his very full lips. "Hand off my boobs!" I whispered. I glanced around, hoping against hope no one had spotted this.

"Correction. Boob, singular," he said.

"Who are you, the grammar police? Hands off!"

"Awfully sorry about that." He removed his hand and stared down at my chest. "Lovely, really. Warm. Soft."

"What?"

"Your breast. From the quick time we've spent together I can tell they're real. Shocking in today's world."

"Right." I glared at the tall man whom I'd just inadvertently gone to second base with. He was handsome as hell, tight, muscular, and I suspected he could have given David Gandy a run for his reign as king of underwear models.

I felt something warm, moist, and sticky in my nether regions and it smelled suspiciously like scotch. I peered down at my rental gown. The skirt was soggy and stained. Blood rushed to my cheeks. I wouldn't be getting my deposit back. "Damn!"

"You have every right to be furious. I wasn't looking where I was going," he said, sliding the tray onto an unoccupied table and snagging a discarded table napkin smeared with remnants of chicken cordon bleu. He dropped to his knees in front of me, dabbing the cloth on my skirt. "I'll fix this."

"No. You're just going to make it worse." I stared down at his thick head of black hair and wide muscular shoulders that strained at the confines of his upscale penguin suit. He worked his way up my shins that had suddenly sprouted goosebumps. "I'll handle it."

"No. *I'll* handle it." He graduated to my thighs. *Pat. Pat. Pat.*

Several wedding guests were watching me.

Getting felt up.

By the persistent hot waiter.

In the middle of the poshest wedding reception of the year.

"Really you don't have to do this," I said. His warm breath penetrated the drenched silk of my gown, heating my skin. My face flushed and I broke into a sweat because in spite of this whole disaster tingles zipped up and down my spine, and this time it wasn't from the Champagne. "Let's just call it a night, okay?"

"That's awfully forward of you," he said. "But if you insist. Your place or mine?"

"That's not what I meant!"

He smiled up at me and my heart melted for a moment. His full lips. His twinkling eyes. The way he waggled his eyebrows in a suggestive, naughty fashion. "I know. Just trying to cheer you up. Can you believe someone actually married John 'Dork' Biltenhouse? I heard a matchmaker fixed them up. Who do you think the idiot was?"

"A very smart idiot." His grip was firm, large fingers pushing through my dress. It felt like he was working. Attempting to accomplish something, righting a wrong, not trying to cop a feel. That said, if this had happened to me on the "L" train, I'd have clocked him over the head with my purse. "Enough. The attendant in the ladies' room can help me—"

"Stop worrying, Cupcake." He winked. "I got this."

"Uh…" He was so earnest, so incredibly gorgeous, that for a second I forgot how to breathe. It dawned on me that waiters weren't usually this hot unless they were struggling actors. I knew only too well how difficult it was to survive in a big city when you were down on your luck, playing a part that you didn't quite have down yet, and my anger dissipated.

Then I wondered if my run in with the hot server was part of my promotion package. Not literally. I didn't work for an escort service after all. But cosmically. Like divine intervention. Life had been super tough the last year and a half. Maybe meeting the sinfully delicious server was the gods' attempts to make up for all the baloney I'd been through.

"What's your name?" he asked.

"Harper. What's yours?"

"You tell me. What name springs to mind when you look at me?" He stared at me with a hint of a smile on his handsome face, the beginning of twinkle wrinkles crinkling around the corners of his eyes. He was so…

"Hot Waiter," I blurted. "Oops! I meant to say… Scott Skater. You look like a Scott Skater to me."

He cocked an eyebrow. "I could swear I've seen you before, Harper. You're so pretty. And boobs that majestic make you impossible to forget."

"Thanks—I think." I reversed my decision and was suddenly tempted to let the excitement of the night take me. Enjoy your night, Harper. Let your guard down and savor an evening of beauty and decadence, fine Champagne, and a gorgeous man who looks like he'd be more than happy to service your every need. "You work at the hotel, right?"

"You could say that."

"I stopped by the catering department with the bride a few months ago when she was sampling entrees for the reception. Maybe you spotted me then." I gazed at his lower lip, full and fleshy, wondering what it would feel like if he kissed me. How it would feel if he'd wrap his big, muscular arm around my shoulders and pulled me to him...

"Harper!" An earnest female voice called, snapping me out of my reverie. I glanced up and spotted my pal, the immaculately coiffed Molly Frankle, waving her hand high in the air as she hustled through the well-appointed crowd toward me.

My heart sank because I realized this stunning man on his knees before me with the big muscular arms, a cleft in his chin, and dark brown hair with a hint of curl at the ends, might have been the handsomest waiter in Chicago, let alone the entire Midwest—but I had to shut this down. "Thank you," I said and popped open the clasp on my pearl-encrusted evening bag, pulled out a twenty bill, and tapped it on his hand that was still attending to my thigh. "I hope this covers the damages."

He stopped and stared up at me. "For what?"

"The drink I spilled."

Molly waved her hands in the air. "Harper! The bride needs you—STAT!"

"I ran into you." He pushed back the bill.

"Clearly, it was the other way around." I extended the twenty.

"It doesn't matter who made first contact, Cupcake. You're doused in Glenfiddich 1962 Private Reserve. You might smell like a trust fund baby after a wild night, but that's an expense you don't want to cover. Besides, I owe you for the dry cleaning."

"You owe me nothing," I said.

He stood up and I was reminded of why I ran into him in the first place. Hot waiter was as big and tall as a Green Bay

Packer linebacker but far prettier. Like a long-lost heir to the Kennedy dynasty. For or a second I wished I was the Harper Emily Schubert from a year ago—a simpler girl living in more innocent times in Oconomowoc, Wisconsin. But innocence had passed me by.

"Harper!" Molly raised her voice, a worried look consuming her face. "I need you!"

"Thanks for the clean-up services," I said. "You're very sweet. But I've got to go."

"You have no idea how sweet I can be," he said. "Stay and find out."

"I wish I could. I really do. But I can't." I turned, my heart bumping around in my chest, and walked away from what could have been my wedding reception fling as the band played *You're Just Too Good to be True.* I stopped in my tracks, and regret nagged at me, practically poking me in the ribs. I couldn't help but wonder what time he got off work.

I turned to look for him. "Hey, I don't even know your real name. What's your name?" But he had vanished into the thick of the wedding crowd. He was so big, a force of nature. How was that even possible?

❦

One click Ms. Match Meets a Millionaire now!

Ms. Match Meets a Millionaire: A Playing Sweeter Romantic Comedy © 2018 Pamela DuMond is a STAND ALONE story, as well as the **sweeter version** of *THE CLIENT* Copyright © 2017 Pamela DuMond - All rights reserved. Publishes early 2018.

BOOKS BY PAMELA DUMOND

'HOT' ROMANCE

21st CENTURY COURTSEAN series

TYCOON: A 21st Century Courtesan Prologue (FREE!)

PLAYER #1

MOVIE STAR #2

BELOVED #3

***

ROYALLY WED ROM-COM series

Part-time Princess #1

Royally Wed #2

Part-time Poser #3

Royally Knocked Up #4

Royally Wed Box Set: Books 1 - 4

***

THE CROWN AFFAIR series

His Sexy Cinderella - A Crown Affair Series Prologue (FREE!)

The Prince's Playbook #1

His Majesty's Measure #2

The American Princess #3

The Duchess's Decision #4

The Crown Affair Collection: Books 1 - 4

The Mortal Beloved Box Set: Books 1 - 3

COZY MYSTERIES

ANNIE GRACELAND COZY MYSTERIES

Cupcakes, Lies, & Dead Guys #1

Cupcakes, Sales, & Cocktails

Cupcakes, Pies, & Hometown Guys

Cupcakes, Paws, & Bad Santa Claus

Cupcakes, Diaries, & Rotten Inquiries

Cupcakes, Bats, & Scaredy Cats

Cupcakes, Bars, & Rock Stars

Cupcakes, Spies, & Despicable Guys

Cupcakes, Screams, & Drama Queens

The Annie Graceland Mystery Collection: Books 1 - 4

The Annie Graceland Mystery Collection #2: Books 5 - 7

FREE

TYCOON: A 21st Century Courtesan Prologue

His Sexy Cinderella - A Crown Affair Series Prologue

SELF-HELP

Staying Young

BOOKS in the WORKS

BELOVED: 21st Century Courtesan #3

HUSBAND: 21st Century Courtesan #4

Cupcakes, Screams, and Drama Queens

For more details please visit Pamela DuMond Author.

ACKNOWLEDGMENTS

Thanks Kelly Hartog for editing. Lori Jackson who rocked the book cover. Thanks Lesley Ann Fogle for rocking the Audible versions of these books.

Thanks to Caitlyn O'Leary, Sylvie Fox, Maggie Marr, and Cindy Sample, and "Pamela's Princesses" for being such awesome cheerleaders. Thanks to my readers and supporters Jeanie Whitmire Jackson, Carolyn Haines, Jennifer Freeman, Carole Sauer, Carrie Hartney, D.C., Cheryl Cavitt Carlson, Colleen Hartney, D.C., Ed Schneider, Joan Brady, Joe Wilson, Kristin Warren, Monica Mason, Cheyenne Mason, Melissa Black Ford, Rita Kempley, to name a few.

A huge thanks to all you readers who encourage me to write more stories. I appreciate all your help. You rock!

I love writing the Royally Wed books and I promise there will be more!

Xo,

Pamela DuMond

ABOUT THE AUTHOR

USA Today Bestselling author of *Part-time Princess* © 2014 and other modern fairytales, Pam writes sexy, steamy, and on occasion silly.

Her books have been optioned for Film/TV, licensed by Chapters Interactive Stories as games, and featured in Glamour UK. A Midwestern girl at heart, Pam landed in L.A. where she says 'No' to kale, 'Yes' to Cardio Barre, and 'What do you want now?' to her two ridiculously cute cats.

Sign up for Pamela DuMond's newsletter.

Like Pamela DuMond Author page on Facebook.

Join the reader group at Pamela DuMond's Dirty Darlings.

Follow Pamela DuMond on Bookbub for timely deals.

Stalk Pamela DuMond on Instagram .

For more information...
www.pameladumond.com

www.ingramcontent.com/pod-product-compliance
Lightning Source LLC
Chambersburg PA
CBHW051944170626
46808CB00007B/2479